thought th

With a move so
happ
and p
touch

'I thi

For a
She c
word
how l
down
the st
fast i
haunt

Desp
beatin
and t
grip.

'Kade
have r

Kade
touch
in fro
of *this*

Bitter
of *thi*
Burqu

Abby Green got hooked on Mills & Boon® romance while still in her teens, when she stumbled across one belonging to her grandmother in the west of Ireland. After many years of reading them voraciously, she sat down one day and gave it a go herself. Happily, after a few failed attempts, Mills & Boon bought her first manuscript.

She works freelance in the film and TV industry, but thankfully the four a.m. starts and the stresses of dealing with recalcitrant actors are becoming more and more infrequent, leaving her more time to write!

She loves to hear from readers, and you can contact her through her website at www.abby-green.com. She lives and works in Dublin.

Recent titles by the same author:

[illegible]TAN'S CHOICE
[illegible] OF THE OASIS

Did you know these are also available as eBooks?
Visit www.millsandboon.co.uk

THE CALL OF THE DESERT

BY

ABBY GREEN

All the characters in this book have no existence outside the imagination of the author, and have no relation whatsoever to anyone bearing the same name or names. They are not even distantly inspired by any individual known or unknown to the author, and all the incidents are pure invention.

First published in Great Britain 2011
by Mills & Boon, an imprint of Harlequin (UK) Limited.
Harlequin (UK) Limited, Eton House, 18-24 Paradise Road,
Richmond, Surrey TW9 1SR

ISBN: 978 0 263 88715 0

Harlequin (UK) policy is to use papers that are natural, renewable and recyclable products and made from wood grown in sustainable forests. The logging and manufacturing process conform to the legal environmental regulations of the country of origin.

Printed and bound in Spain
by Blackprint CPI, Barcelona

THE CALL OF THE DESERT

This is for India Grey, Natalie Rivers
and Heidi Rice—I couldn't do this job without any of
you, and it wouldn't be half as much fun. Thank you.

(My phone company also extends its thanks
for keeping them in business.)

CHAPTER ONE

“THE Emir of Burquat. His Royal Highness Sheikh Kaden Bin Rashad al Abbas.”

Kaden looked out over the thronged ballroom in London’s exclusive Royal Archaeology Club. Everyone was staring at him and a hush had descended on the crowd, but that didn’t bother Kaden. He was used to such attention.

He walked down the ornate marble steps, one hand in his trouser pocket, watching dispassionately as people were caught staring and turned away hurriedly again. Well, to be more accurate, the men turned away and the women’s looks lingered—some blatantly so. Like that of the buxom waitress who was waiting at the bottom of the stairs to hand him a glass of champagne. She smiled coquettishly as he took the glass but Kaden had already looked away; she was far too young for his jaded heart and soul.

Ever since he’d been a teenager he’d been aware he possessed a certain power when it came to women. When he looked in the mirror, though, and saw his own harsh features staring back at him, he wondered cynically if all they felt was the seductive urge to wipe away that cynicism and replace it with something softer. He had been softer…once. But it was so long ago now that he could hardly remember what it had felt like. It was like a dream, and perhaps like all dreams it had never been real.

Just then a movement on the other side of the room caught his eye, and a glimpse of a shiny blonde head among all the darker ones had his insides contracting. *Still. Even now.* He cursed himself and welcomed the sight of the club's managing director hurrying towards him, wondering angrily why he hadn't yet mastered such arbitrarily reflexive responses to the memory of something that had only ever been as flimsy as a dream.

Julia Somerton's heart was palpitating, making her feel a little dizzy.

Kaden.

Here.

In the same room.

He'd descended the stairs and disappeared into the throng of people, despite his superior height. But that first image of him, appearing in the doorway like some sleek, dark-haired god, would be etched on her retina for ever. It was an image that was already carved indelibly onto her heart. The part of her heart that she couldn't erase him from, no matter how much she tried or how much time passed.

She'd noted several things in the space of that heart-stopping split second when she'd heard his name being called and had looked up. He was still as stupendously gorgeous as he'd been when she'd first met him. Tall, broad and dark, with the exotic appeal of someone not from these lands—someone who had been carved out of a much more arid and unforgiving place. He'd been too far away for her to see him in any detail, but even from where she'd stood she'd felt the impact of that black gaze—eyes so dark you could lose yourself for ever. *And hadn't she once?*

Some small, detached part of herself marvelled that he could have such an effect on her after all this time. Twelve long years. She was a divorcée now, a million miles from the idealistic girl she'd once been. When she'd known him.

The last time she'd seen Kaden she'd just turned twenty—weeks before his own twentieth birthday. Something she'd used to tease him mercilessly about: being with an *older woman*.

Her heart clenched so violently that she put a hand to her chest, and one of her companions said with concern, "Julia, dear, are you all right? You've gone quite pale."

She shook her head, and placed her drink down on a nearby table with a sweaty hand. Her voice came out husky, rough, "It must be the heat… I'll just get some air for a minute."

Blindly Julia made her way through the crowd, pushing, not looking left or right, heading for where patio doors led out to a terrace which overlooked manicured gardens. She only vaguely heard her colleague call after her, "Don't go too far—you've got to say your piece soon!"

When she finally reached the doors and stepped out, she sucked in huge lungfuls of air. She felt shaky and jelly-like—at a remove from everything. She recognised shock. It was mid-August and late evening. The city air was heavy and oppressively warm. The faintly metallic scent of a storm was in the atmosphere. Huge clouds sat off in the distance, as if waiting for their cue to roll in. The garden here was famous for its exotic species of plants which had been brought back by many an adventurer and nurtured over the years by the dedicated gardeners.

But Julia was blind to all that.

Her hands gripped the wall so hard her knuckles shone white in the gathering twilight. She was locked in a whirlpool of memories, so many memories, and they were as bright and as painfully bittersweet as if it had all happened yesterday.

Ridiculously tears pricked her eyes, and an awful sense of loss gripped her. Yet how could this be? She was a thirty-two-year-old woman. Past her prime, many people would say, or perhaps coming into it, others would maintain. She felt past her prime. The day she'd flown away from the Emirate of Burquat on the Arabian Peninsula something inside her had withered and died. And even though she'd got on with her studies and surpassed her own dreams to gain a master's degree and a doctorate, and had married and loved her husband in her own way, she'd never truly *felt* again. The reason for that was in the room behind her, a silent malevolent presence.

God, she'd loved him so much—

"Dr Somerton, it's time for your speech."

An urgent voice jarred her out of the memories. Dredging up strength from somewhere deep inside her, from a place she hadn't needed to visit in a long time, Julia steeled herself and turned around. She was going to have to stand up in front of all these people and speak for fifteen minutes, all the while knowing he was there, watching her.

Remembering?

Perhaps he wouldn't even remember… Perhaps he'd struggle to place her in his past. Her mouth became a bitter line. He'd certainly had enough women to make her blur into the crowd—not to mention a marriage of his own. She hated to admit that she was as aware of his exploits as the next person on the street who read the gossip rags on their lunchbreaks.

Maybe he'd wonder why she looked familiar. Acute pain gripped her and she repressed it brutally. Perhaps he wouldn't remember the long nights in the desert when it had felt as if they were the only two people in the world underneath a huge blanket of stars. Perhaps he wouldn't remember the beautiful poignancy of becoming each other's first lover and how their naïve lovemaking had quickly developed beyond naivetée to pure passion and an insatiable need for one another.

Perhaps he wouldn't remember when he'd said to her one night: "*I will love you always. No other woman could ever claim my heart the way you have.*"

And perhaps he wouldn't remember that awful day in the beautiful Royal Palace in Burquat when he'd become someone cold and distant and cruel.

Reassuring herself that a man like Kaden would have consigned her to the dust heap of his memories, and stifling the urge to run from the room, Julia pasted a smile on her face and followed her colleague back into the crowd, trying desperately to remember what on earth she was supposed to talk about.

"Ah, Sheikh Kaden, there you are. Dr Julia Somerton is just about to speak. I believe she used her research in Burquat for her masters degree. Perhaps you met her all those years ago? She's involved in fundraising now, for various worldwide archaeological projects."

Kaden looked at the red-faced man who'd forced his way through the crowd to come and join him, and made a non-committal response. The man was the managing director of the club, who had invited him with a view to wooing funds out of him. Kaden was trying to disguise the uncomfortable jolt of shock to hear the name *Julia*. Despite the fact that he'd never met another Julia in Burquat, he told himself that there might have been another student by that name and he wouldn't have necessarily been aware, considering his lack of interest in all things archaeological after *she'd* left.

This was his first foray back into that world and it would be ironic in the extreme if he was to meet *her*. She had been Julia Connors, not Somerton. Although, as an inner voice pointed out, she could be married by now. In fact, why wouldn't she be? *He* had been married, after all. At the memory of his marriage Kaden felt the usual cloud of black anger threaten to overwhelm him. He resolutely pushed it aside. He was not one to dwell on the past.

And yet one aspect of his past which had refused to dissolve into the mists of time was facing him right now. If it *was* her. Unaccountably his heart picked up pace.

A hush descended over the crowd. Kaden looked towards the front of the room and the world halted on its axis for a terrifying moment when he saw the slim woman in the black cocktail dress ascending the steps to the podium. *It was her.* Julia. In a split second he was transported back to the moment when he'd realised that, because of lust, he'd placed her on a pedestal that she had no right to grace. And only that realisation had stopped him making the biggest mistake of his life.

Shaking his mind free of the disturbingly vivid memory, Kaden narrowed his eyes on Julia. Her voice was husky; it had caught him from the first moment they'd met. She'd been wearing a T-shirt and dusty figure-hugging jeans. Her long hair had fallen in bright tendrils over her shoulders. A safari-style hat had shaded her face from the sun. Her figure had been lithe and so effortlessly sensual he'd lost the power of speech.

If anything she was more beautiful than that first day he'd seen her. Time had hollowed out her cheeks, adding an angularity that hadn't been there before. *She'd only been nineteen.* Her face had still held a slight hint of puppy-plumpness. As had her body. From what he could see now, she looked slimmer, with a hint of enticing cleavage just visible in the V of her dress. In fact there was a fragility about her that hadn't been there before.

She was a million miles from that first tantalising dusty image he held in his mind's eye; she was elegance personified now, with her long blonde hair pulled back into a low ponytail. The heavy side parting swept it across her forehead and down behind one ear. Her groomed appearance was doing little, though, to stop the torrent of carnal images flooding Kaden's mind—and in such lurid detail that his body started to harden in response.

He would have anticipated that she'd have no effect on him. Much like any ex-lover. But the opposite was true. This was inconceivable. He had to concede now, with extreme reluctance, that no woman since this woman had exerted such a sensual hold over him. He'd never again lost control as he had with her—every time.

And he'd never felt the same acrid punch of jealousy to his gut as when he'd seen her in another man's arms, with another man's mouth on hers, tasting her…feeling her soft curves pressed against him. The vividness of that emotion was dizzying in its freshness, and he fought to negate it, too stunned by its resurgence to look too closely into what it meant.

This woman had been a valuable lesson in never allowing his base nature to rule his head or his heart again. Yet the years of wielding that control felt very flimsy how he was faced with her again.

More than a little bewildered at this onslaught of memories, and irrationally angry that she was here to precipitate them, Kaden felt his whole body radiate displeasure. Just then a rumble of laughter trickled through the gathered crowd in reaction to something she'd said. Kaden's mouth tightened even more, and with that tension making his movements jerky he said something about getting some air and stalked towards the open patio doors.

As soon as Julia's speech was over he was going to get out of there and forget that he'd ever seen her again.

Julia stepped down off the dais. She'd faltered during her speech for long seconds when she'd noticed Kaden head and shoulders above the rest of the crowd, at the back of the room like a forbidding presence, those dark eyes boring through her. And then with an abrupt move he'd moved outside. Almost as if disgusted by something she'd said. It had taken all her powers of concentration to keep going, and she'd used up all her reserves.

To her abject relief she saw her boss at the fundraising foundation come towards her. He put a hand to her elbow and for once she wasn't concerned about keeping distance between them. Ever since her divorce had come through a year ago Nigel had been making his interest clear, despite Julia's clear lack of encouragement. Tonight, though, she needed all the support she could get. If she could just get through the rest of the relentless schmoozing and get out of there perhaps she could pretend she'd never seen Kaden.

Nigel was babbling excitedly about something as he steered her away, but she couldn't even hear him above the din of chatter and the clink of glasses. People were making the most of the *gratis* champagne reception. Julia craved that sweet oblivion, but it was not to be.

With dread trickling into her veins and her belly hollowing out, she could already see where they were headed—towards someone at the back of the room, near the terrace. Someone with his back to them: tall, broad and powerful. Thick ebony-black hair curled a touch too much over the collar of his jacket, exactly the way it had when she'd first met him.

Like a recalcitrant child she tried to dig her heels into the ground, but Nigel was blithely unaware, whispering confidentially, "He's an emir, so I'm not sure how you have to address him. Maybe call him Your Highness just in case. It would be such a coup to interest him in the foundation."

In that split second Julia had a flashback to when she'd met Kaden for the first time. She'd only been working on the dig for a couple of weeks, had still been getting used to the intense heat, when a pair of shoes had come into her line of vision. She'd barely looked up.

"*Don't* step there. Whoever you are. You're about to walk on top of a fossil that's probably in the region of three thousand years old."

The shoe had hovered in mid-air and come back down again in a safer spot, and a deep, lightly accented voice had drawled seductively, "Do you always greet people with such enthusiasm?"

Julia gritted her teeth. Since she'd arrived she'd been the object of intense male interest and speculation. She was under no illusions that it was most likely because she was blonde and the only female under fifty on the dig. "If you don't mind, I'm in the middle of something here."

The shoes didn't move and the voice came again, sounding much more arrogant and censorious. "I *do* mind, actually—I am the Crown Prince and you will acknowledge me when I speak to you."

She'd completely forgotten that the Emir was due to visit with some important guests that day—and *his son.* Dismay filling Julia, she put down her brush and finally looked up, and up, and up again, to see a tall, broad figure standing over her. The sun was in her eyes so all she could make out was his shape—which was formidable.

Taking off her gloves, she slowly stood, and came face to face with the most handsome man she'd ever seen in her life. Robes highlighted his awe-inspiring height and broad shoulders. He wore a turban, but that couldn't hide the jet-black hair curling down to his collar, or the square cut of his jaw. The most mesmerising dark eyes.

Feeling more than a little overwhelmed she took off her hat and held out her hand…

"And this is Dr Somerton, who you just heard. As our

funds manager she's been instrumental in making sure that funding reaches our digs all over the world."

Past merged into present and Julia found that she was holding out her hand in an automatic response to the introduction. She was now facing Kaden, and much as she'd have loved to avert her gaze he took up a lot of space, completely arresting in a dark suit with a snowy-white shirt open at the neck, making him stand out from the men in the crowd who were more formally dressed. He looked darker, and infinitely more dangerous than any other man there.

There was no such thing as sliding towards middle age with a receding hairline and expanding gut for him. He oozed virility, vitality, and a heady, earthy sexual magnetism far more powerful than she remembered. There was not a hint of softness about him, or his face. He was all lean angles. The blade of his slightly crooked nose highlighted a sense of danger and a man in his vigorous prime. She remembered the day he'd got that injury, while playing his country's brutal national game.

Her heart squeezed as she recalled that moment and saw the new harshness stamping the lines of his face. She wondered how long it had been there. Her eyes slid down helplessly…his mouth hadn't changed. It was as sensual as she remembered, with its full lower lip and the slightly thinner, albeit beautifully shaped upper lip. She'd used to love tracing that line with her finger. Heat flared in her belly. *And with her tongue*. It was a mouth which held within it the power to inspire a need in the most cynical of women to make this man *hers*.

The strength of that need washed through Julia, and dismay gripped her. She couldn't still want this man—not after all these years. Her hand hovered in mid-air as the moment stretched out between them. He was looking at her as intently as she was looking at him, but it was no consolation. There was no polite spark of recognition, only an extreme air of tension. He knew her, but clearly did not relish meeting her again.

Julia realised that just as his big hand enveloped her much smaller one, and a million and one sensations exploded throughout her body.

Far too innately civilised to be deliberately rude and ignore Julia's hand, as he perversely longed to do, Kaden reached out to take it. He instinctively gritted his jaw against the inevitable physical contact but it was no good. At the first touch of his fingers to that small, soft hand he wanted to slide his thumb with sensual intent along the gap between her thumb and forefinger in a lover's caress. He wanted to curl his fingers around her palm and feel every delicate bone.

He wanted to relearn this woman in an erotic way that was so forceful it set off a maelstrom of biblical proportions inside him. And somewhere in his head he wondered when had just shaking a woman's hand ever precipitated such an onslaught of need.

A voice answered him: about twelve years ago, in the searing heat of the afternoon sun amongst dusty relics, when this same woman had stood before him with a shy smile on her face, her hand in his. And, much to his chagrin, Kaden felt his intention to walk away and forget he'd seen her again dissolve in a rush of lust.

CHAPTER TWO

A MINOR earthquake was taking place within Julia's body, and Kaden seemed loath to let her hand go—about as reluctant as she was for him to let it go. The realisation shamed her, and yet to her horror she couldn't seem to muster up the energy to extricate her hand from his. She noticed the look in his eyes change to something ambiguous, and every cell in her blood jumped and fizzed in reaction.

An emotion which felt awfully poignant and *yearning* was threatening. She struggled to remember where she was, and with whom, but it was almost impossible. The reality that it was *Kaden* in front of her was too much to take in. All she could do was react.

As suddenly as Julia had registered the changed intensity in Kaden's gaze locked onto hers it was gone, and his eyes moved to take in their companions. Julia had forgotten all about them. Her hand was dropped as summarily as if he had flung it away from him, and a dark cloud of foreboding seemed to blot out the sultry evening just visible through the open patio doors. She shivered in response, and wanted to hug her arms around her body.

Nigel was saying nervously, "His Royal Highness the

Emir of Burquat," and Julia was wondering a little hysterically if she should be curtseying. She didn't trust her voice to speak and then Kaden's black gaze was back on her.

"Dr Somerton."

His voice was so achingly familiar that she longed to be able to hold onto something for balance, only dimly registering the cool tone.

A small anxious-looking man with a red face was beside Kaden. Julia recognised him as the director of the club. He was talking, but his voice seemed to be coming from far away,

"Perhaps you have met before, Doctor? When you were in Burquat during your studies?"

A sharp pain lanced Julia and she looked at Kaden, not sure what to say.

His mouth turned up in a parody of a smile and he drawled, "I seem to have some vague recollection. What year were you there?"

The slap of rejection was so strong it almost made Julia take a step back. The awful sense of isolation she'd felt when she'd left Burquat was as fresh now as twelve years ago. That this man could transport her so easily back to those painful emotions was devastating. Perhaps he could tell just how excruciating this was for her—hadn't she all but thrown herself at him that last day? Perhaps he thought he was sparing her some embarrassment now?

She forced an equally polite and distant smile to her lips. "It's so long ago now I can barely recall it myself."

She switched her brittle-feeling smile to the other men. "Gentlemen, if you don't need me for this discussion I'd appreciate it if you would excuse me. I just got back from New York this afternoon, and I'm afraid the jet lag is catching up with me."

"Your husband is waiting for you at home? Or perhaps he's here in the room?"

Shock at the bluntness of Kaden's question slammed into Julia. How dared he all but pretend not to know her and then ask such a pointedly personal question? Her jaw felt tight. "For your information, *Your Highness*, I am no longer married. My husband and I are divorced."

Kaden did not like the surge of emotion that ripped through him at her curt answer. He had had an image of her returning to a cosy home to be greeted by some faceless man and had felt a blackness descend over his vision, forcing him to ask the question. Even realising that, he couldn't stop himself asking, "So why are you still using your married name?"

Julia's face tightened. "I'm involved in various contracts and it's simply been easier to leave it for the moment. I have every intention of changing it back in the future."

It was as if Kaden was enclosed in a bubble with this woman. The other men went unnoticed, forgotten. Unbidden and unwelcome emotion was clouding everything.

At that moment Nigel, Julia's boss, moved perceptibly closer to her, taking her elbow in his hand, staking a very public claim.

Only moments ago she'd welcomed his support and his tacit interest as a barrier. Now Julia chafed and made a jerky move away, causing Nigel's hand to drop. She could feel his wounded look without even seeing it, and her head began to throb. The club's director who still stood beside Kaden, was looking a bit bewildered at the obvious tension in the air, which was making a lie of the fact that she and Kaden claimed to barely know one another.

She knew she'd only been introduced as a polite formality. She wasn't expected to take part in Nigel's wooing of new donors. Her job started when they had to decide how those funds would be best used. If she'd known for a second that Kaden was due to be here this evening, she would have made certain not to come.

Determined to succeed this time, Julia stepped away from the trio of men on very shaky legs. "Please, gentlemen—if you'll excuse me?"

Ignoring the dagger looks from Nigel, and the dark condemnation emanating from Kaden like a physical force, she turned on her heel and walked away. It seemed to take an age to get through the crowd. She was almost at the door when she felt a hand on her arm, but it didn't induce anything more than irritation and she reluctantly turned to face Nigel. His handsome face was red.

"Are you going to tell me what that was all about?"

Once again Julia pulled her arm free and kept walking. "It was about nothing, Nigel. I'm tired and I want to go home, that's all."

She hoped the panic she felt at being there for one second longer than was absolutely necessary didn't come through in her voice. She reached the cloakroom and handed in the ticket for her jacket, noticing a visible tremor in her hand.

"So you two obviously know each other, then? I'd have to be deaf, dumb and blind to fail to notice *that* atmosphere."

Julia sighed. "We knew each other a long time ago, Nigel." She turned and put on her jacket, which had just been handed to her, and pointed out gently, "Not that it's any of your business."

His face became mottled. "It *is* my business when the most potentially lucrative donor we've had in years could get scared off because he's had some kind of previous relationship with my funds manager."

Julia stopped and faced Nigel, forcing herself to stay civil. "I'm sure he's mature enough not to let a tiny incident like this change his mind about donating funds to research. Anyway, it's all the more reason for me to leave and stay out of your way."

She turned to go and Nigel caught her hand. Gritting her teeth at his persistence, Julia turned back, her stomach churning slightly at the sweaty grip of his hand—so far removed from the cool yet hot touch from Kaden.

He was conciliatory. "Look, I'm sorry, Julia. Forgive me? Let me take you out to dinner this week."

Julia fought back the urge to say yes, which would be the easy thing to do, to placate him. Seeing Kaden had upset any equilibrium she thought she might have attained since her divorce had become final. Since she had last seen *him*. And that knowledge was too frightening to take in fully.

She shook her head, "I'm sorry, Nigel. I have thought about it...and I'm just not ready for dating." She pulled her hand from his and backed away. "I'm really sorry. I'll see you tomorrow in the office." Already she could imagine his sulky mood at being turned down and dreaded it.

She turned and walked quickly to the door. Her heart was hammering, and all she wanted was to escape to the quiet solace of her house where she could get out of her tailored dress and curl up. She wanted to block out the evening's events and the fact that her past had rushed up to meet her with the force of a sledgehammer blow.

As soon as Julia had turned and walked away Kaden should have been putting her out of his mind and focusing on the business at hand, as he would have with any other ex-lover. But he wasn't. He found that the urge to go after her was nigh on impossible to resist. Especially when that obsequious man who'd had the temerity to put his hand on her had followed her like a besotted lap dog.

Kaden made his excuses to the still bewildered-looking director of the club and forged his way through the crowd, ignoring the not so hushed whispers as he passed people by. His blood was humming. He felt curiously euphoric, and also uncultivated—like a predator in the desert, an eagle soaring high who had spotted its prey and would not rest until it was caught.

It was an uncomfortable reminder of how he'd felt from the moment he'd first met Julia, when sanity had taken a hike and he'd given himself over to a dream as dangerous as any opiate could induce. But this feeling was too strong to deny or rationalise.

The fact that she represented a lapse in emotional control he'd never allowed again only caught up with him when he reached the lobby and saw it was empty.

She'd disappeared.

So what was this desolation that swept through him? And what was this rampant need clawing through him to find her again? He was done with Julia. He'd been done with her a long time ago.

Disgusted with himself for this lapse, Kaden called up his security, determined to get out of there and do what he'd set out to do all along: forget that he'd ever seen Julia Connors—he scowled, *Somerton*—again.

He had no desire to revisit a time when he'd come very close to letting his heart rule his head, forgetting all about duty and responsibility in the pursuit of personal fulfilment. He didn't have that luxury. He'd *never* had that luxury.

Julia could see the tube station entrance ahead of her, not far from the building she'd just left behind. The night-time London air was unbearably heavy around her now, making a light sweat break out over her skin and on the nape of her neck under her hair. Thunder rolled ominously in the distance. A storm had been threatening all evening, and if she'd been in better humour she might have appreciated the symbolism. The clouds that had been squatting in the distance were now firmly overhead—low, dark and menacing.

What was making the weather feel even more ominous was the fact that she'd been having disturbing dreams of Kaden lately. Maybe, she wondered a little hysterically, she was hallucinating?

Hesitating for a moment, Julia stopped and looked back. But the building just sat there, innocently benign, lights blazing from the windows, laughter trickling out into the quiet street from the party. She shuddered despite the heat. She wasn't going back now anyway. She couldn't face Nigel again. *Or* Kaden's coolly sardonic demeanour. As if nothing had ever happened between them.

Part of her longed to just jump in a cab, but her inherently frugal nature forbade it. Out of the corner of her eye she saw a sleek black shape slow to a crawl alongside her—just before she heard the accompanying low hum of a very expensive engine. At the same time as she turned automatically to look, lightning forked in the sky and the heavens opened. She was comprehensively drenched within seconds, but had become rooted to the spot.

Everything seemed to happen in slow motion as she registered the Royal Burquati flag on the bonnet of the car. She noticed the tinted windows, and the equally sleek accompanying Jeep, which had to be carrying the ubiquitous security team.

As she stood there getting soaked, unable to move, Julia was helplessly transported back to a moment in the hot, winding, ancient streets of Burquat City, when, breathless with laughter, her hand clamped in Kaden's, they'd escaped from his bodyguards into a private walled garden. There, he'd pushed her up against a wall, taken away the veil hiding her face, and kissed her for the first time.

It was only when the back door of the car opened near her and she saw the tall figure of Kaden emerge that reality rushed back. Along with it came her breath and her heartbeat, and the knowledge that she hadn't been hallucinating.

The rain seemed to bounce off him, spraying droplets into a halo around him. The sky was apocalyptic behind him. And still that rain was beating down.

Julia backed away, her eyes glued to him as if mesmerised.

"Julia. Let me give you a lift."

Her name on his tongue with that exotic accent did funny things to her insides. A strangled half-laugh came out of Julia's mouth. "A lift?" She shook her head, "I don't need a lift—I need to go home. I'll take the tube."

She dragged her gaze from his and finally managed to turn around. Only to feel her arm caught in a hard grip. Electric tingles shot up and down her arm and into her groin just as more lightning lit up the sky. She looked up at Kaden, who had come to stand in front of her. So close that she could see his jet-black hair plastered to his skull, that awesomely beautiful face. Those black eyes. Rain ran in rivulets down the lean planes, over hard cheekbones.

"What do you want, Kaden? Or should I address you by your full title?" Bitterness and something much scarier made her feel emotional. "You gave a very good impression back there of not knowing who I was. I'm surprised you even remember my name."

Through the driving rain she could see his jaw clench at that. His black gaze swept her up and down. Then his hand gentled on her arm, and perversely that made her feel even shakier. With something she couldn't decipher in his voice he said, "I remember your name, Julia." And then, with easy solicitude, "You're soaked through. And now I'm soaked. My apartment isn't far from here. Let me take you there so you can dry off."

Panic mixed with something much more hot and primal clutched Julia's gut. Go with Kaden to his apartment? To *dry off*? She remembered the way his look had changed earlier to something ambiguous. It was a long time since she'd felt that curl of hot desire in her abdomen, and to be reminded of how this man had been the only one ever to precipitate it was galling. And that he could still make it happen twelve years on was even more disturbing.

She shook her head and tried to extricate her arm. "No, thank you. I don't want to put you out of your way."

His jaw clenched again. "Do you really want to sit on a tube dripping wet and walk home like a drowned rat?"

Instantly she felt deflated. She could well imagine that she *did* resemble a drowned rat. Mascara must be running down her cheeks in dark rivers. He was just being polite—had probably seen her and hadn't wanted to appear rude by driving past. His convoy would have been far too conspicuous to go unnoticed.

"I can take a taxi if I need to. Why are you doing this?"

He shrugged minutely. "I wasn't expecting to see you…it's been a surprise."

She all but snorted. It certainly was. She had no doubt that he'd never expected to see her again in his lifetime. And thinking of that now—how close she'd come to never seeing him again—Julia felt an aching sense of loss grip her. And urgency. She wouldn't see Kaden after tonight. She knew that. This was a fluke, a monumental coincidence. He was just curious—perhaps intrigued.

He'd been her first lover. Her first love. *Her only love*?

Before she could quash that disturbing thought Kaden was manoeuvring her towards the open door of his car, as if some tacit acquiescence had passed between them. Julia felt weak for not protesting, but she knew in that moment that she didn't have the strength to just walk away. Because meeting him again *didn't* mean nothing to her.

He handed her into the plush interior of the luxury car and came around the other side. Once his large, rangy body was settled in the back seat alongside her he isued a terse command in Arabic, and the car pulled off so smoothly that Julia only knew they were moving because the tube station passed them in a blaze of refracted light through the driving rain.

Kaden sat back and looked over at Julia. He could see her long dark lashes. Her nose had the tiniest bump, which gave her profile an aquiline look, and her mouth…

He used to study this woman's mouth for hours. Obsessed with its shape, its full lower lip and the perfect curve of its bow-shaped upper lip. He'd once known this profile as well as his own. *Better.*

She wore a light jacket, but the rain had made her clothes heavy and the V in the neckline of the dress was being dragged downwards to reveal the pale swells of her breasts. He could see a tantalising hint of the black lace of her bra, and evidence of her agitation as her chest rose and fell with quick breaths.

Rage at his uncharacteristic lack of control rose high. He'd fully intended to leave and put her out of his mind, but then he'd seen her walking along the street, with that quick, efficient walk he remembered. Not artful or practised, but completely sensuous all the same. As if she was unconscious of how sexy she was. He'd forgotten that a woman could be unconsciously sexy. Before he'd known what he was doing, he'd found himself instructing his driver to stop the car.

Sexual awareness stunned him anew. It shouldn't be so overwhelmingly fresh. As if they'd hardly been apart. For a long time after she'd left Burquat Kaden had told himself that his inability to forget about her was because of the fact that she'd been his first lover, and that brought with it undeniable associations and indelible memories.

But he couldn't deny as he sat there now, with this carnal *heat* throbbing between them, that the pleasure they'd discovered together had been more than just the voluptuous delight of new lovers discovering unfamiliar terrain. It had been as intensely mind—blowing as anything he'd experienced since. And sitting beside Julia was effortlessly shattering any illusion he'd entertained that he'd been the one to control his response to women in the intervening years. They just hadn't been *her*. That knowledge was more than cataclysmic.

Julia could feel Kaden's eyes on her, but she was determined not to look at him. When they'd been together he'd always had a way of looking at her so intently…as if he wanted to devour her whole. It had thrilled her and scared her a little in equal measure. His intensity had been so dark and compelling. She'd felt the lash of that dark intensity when it had been turned against her.

If she turned and saw that look now…

She raised her hand to her neck in a nervous reflex and felt that it was bare. The wave of relief that coursed through her when she realised what she'd just done was nothing short of epic. She always wore a gold necklace with the detail of an intricate love knot at its centre. It had been bought from a stall in the souk in Burquat. But its main significance was that Kaden had bought it for her, and despite what had happened between them she still wore it every day—apart from when she was travelling, for fear of losing it.

The only reason she wasn't wearing it now was because she'd been in such a rush earlier, upon returning from the US, that she'd forgotten to put it back on. The knowledge burned within her, because she knew that it somehow symbolised her link to this man when no link existed any more. If he had seen the necklace— Her mind seized at the prospect. It would have been like wearing a badge saying *You still mean something to me.* And she was only realising herself, here and now, how shamefully true that was.

"We're here."

The car was drawing to a smooth halt outside an exclusive-looking building. A liveried doorman was hurrying over to open the car door, and before Julia knew it she was standing on the pavement watching as Kaden came to join her. The rain had become a light drizzle, and Julia shivered in clothes that felt uncomfortably damp against her skin, despite the heavy warmth of the night.

Kaden ushered Julia in through the open doors. The doorman bowed his head deferentially as they passed. Julia felt numb inside and out. Shock was spreading, turning her into some sort of automaton. Sleek doors were opening, and then they were standing in an opulently decorated lift. The doors closed again, and with a soft jolt they were ascending.

A sense of panic was rising as she stood in that confined space next to Kaden's formidable presence, but before she could do anything the door was opening again and Julia was being led straight from the lift into what had to be the penthouse apartment. It was an old building, but the apartment had obviously been refitted and it oozed sleek modernity with an antique twist. It was decorated in understated tones of cream and gold, effortlessly luxurious. The tall windows showcased the glittering city outside as Kaden led her into a huge reception room and turned to face her.

Julia looked away from the windows to catch Kaden's

dark gaze making a leisurely return up her body. Heat exploded in her belly, and when his eyes met hers again she found it hard to breathe.

He backed away to an open door on the other side of the room and said coolly, "There is a bedroom and *en suite* bathroom through here, if you want to freshen up and get dry."

Julia followed his tall form, feeling very bedraggled. She was aware of trailing water all over the luxurious carpet. He turned again at the open door, through which she could see a set of rooms—a smaller sitting room leading into a bedroom.

"I'll have your clothes attended to if you leave them in the sitting room."

Julia looked at him, and a curious kind of relief went through her. "You have a housekeeper here?"

Kaden shook his head, "No, but someone will attend to them, and I'll leave some dry clothes out for you."

How could she have forgotten the myriad silent servants who were always present to do the royal bidding, no matter what it was? Like erecting exotic Bedouin tents in the desert in a matter of hours, just for them. Her belly cramped. Still in a state of shock, she could only nod silently and watch as Kaden strode away and left her alone.

She walked through the opulent rooms until she came to the bedroom, where she carefully closed the door behind her, leaning back against it. She grimaced at herself. Kaden was hardly likely to bash the door down because he was so consumed with uncontrollable lust. She could well imagine that his tastes no longer ran to wet and bedraggled archaeologists.

Shaking her head, as if that might shake some sanity

back into it, she kicked off her shoes and pushed away from the door. She explored the bathroom, which held a glorious sunken bath and huge walk-in shower. She caught a glimpse of herself in the mirror and her eyes grew big. She did indeed look as if she'd been dragged through a hedge backwards and then hosed down with water. Her long blonde hair hung in rats' tails over her shoulders and was stuck to her head. Mascara had made huge dark smudges under her eyes.

With a scowl at herself, she peeled off her drenched clothes. She got a towel from the bathroom to protect the soft furnishings and left them in the outer sitting room, half terrified that Kaden would walk back through the door at any moment. She scuttled back through the bedroom into the bathroom. With a towel wrapped around her she gave a longing glance to the bath, but stepped into the shower instead. Taking a bath in Kaden's apartment felt far too decadent a thing to do.

As it was, just standing naked under the powerful hot spray of water felt illicit and wicked. To know that Kaden was mere feet away in another room…also naked under a hot shower… With a groan of disgust at her completely inappropriate imagination, Julia turned her face upwards. She resolved to get re-dressed in her wet clothes if she had to, and then get out of there as fast as she could.

Kaden had showered and changed into dry clothes, and now stood outside the rooms he'd shown Julia into. He dithered. He never dithered, but all he could see in his mind's eye was the seductive image of Julia standing before him in those wet clothes. She should have looked like a drowned rat, but she hadn't. That cool, classic

English beauty stood out a mile—along with the delicate curves of her breasts, waist and hips.

The burning desire he'd felt in the car hadn't abated one bit, and normally when he was attracted to a woman it was a straightforward affair. But this wasn't just some random woman. This woman came with long silken ties to the past. *To his heart.* He rejected that rogue thought outright. She'd never affected his heart. He'd thought she had…but it had been lust. Overwhelming, yes, but just lust. Not love.

He'd learnt young not to trust romantic love. His father had married for love. But after his mother had died in childbirth with his younger sister his father had silently communicated to him that love only brought pain. It had been there in the way that his father had become a shadow of his former self, wrapped up in grief and solitude. Kaden had always been made very aware that one day he would rule his country, so he could never afford to let such frivolous emotions overwhelm *him* the way they'd taken over his father's life.

Kaden's father had married again, but this time for all the *expected* reasons. Practicality and lineage. Unfortunately his second wife had been cold and manipulative, further compounding Kaden's negative impressions of marriage and love. Any halcyon memories he might have had of his mother and father being happy together had quickly faded into something that felt like a wispy dream—unreal.

Yet when Kaden had met Julia he'd been seduced into forgetting everything he'd learnt. Guilt weighed heavily on him even now. And that sense of betrayal. If he hadn't seen her with that other man…if he hadn't realised how fickle she was…

Kaden cursed himself for this sudden introspection.

In his hands he held some dry clothes. He knocked lightly and heard nothing. So he went in. The bedroom was dimly lit and the door to the bathroom was slightly open. As if in a trance he walked further into the bedroom and laid the dry clothes down on the bed. He'd picked up Julia's wet clothes on the way through. Her scent hit his nostrils now and his eyes closed. Still the same distinctive lavender scent. A dart of anger rose up, as if her scent was mocking him by not having changed.

Before his mind could become clouded with evocative memories a sound made him open his eyes to see Julia, framed in the doorway of the bathroom, with only a towel wrapped around her body and another towel turban—like on her head. Steam billowed out behind her, bringing with it that delicate scent.

Lust slammed into Kaden like a two-ton lorry. Right in his solar plexus. Long shapely legs were bare, so were pale shoulders and arms. Kaden cursed himself for bringing her here. The last thing he needed right now was to be reopening doors best left shut.

He said, with a cool bite in his voice, "I'll send these out to be dried." He indicated the clothes on the bed, "You can change into these for now. They should fit."

Julia's eyes, which had widened on seeing him, moved to the clothes on the bed. He saw her tense perceptibly. She shook her head, a flush coming into her cheeks, and put out a hand. "I'll change back into my own clothes and go home."

An image of her walking out through the door made Kaden's self-recrimination dissolve in an instant. He held the clothes well out of Julia's reach. "Don't be silly. You'll get pneumonia if you put these back on."

Julia's eyes narrowed and she stretched her hand out more. "Really—I don't mind. This wasn't a good idea. I should never have agreed to come here."

CHAPTER THREE

SILENCE thickened and grew between them. Julia couldn't fathom what was going on behind those darker than dark eyes. And then Kaden moved towards her and she stepped back. Her heart nearly jumped out of her chest.

He pointed out silkily, "But you did come. What are you afraid of, Julia? That you won't be able to control yourself around me?"

A few seconds ago she'd seen a look of something like cool distaste cross his face, and yet now he was acknowledging the heat between them. Baiting her. Her heart was thumping so hard she felt sure it would be evident through the towel wrapped around her.

A long buried sensation rushed through her like a tangible force—what it had felt like to have his naked body between her legs, thrusting into her with awesome strength.

For a moment she couldn't breathe, then she said threadily, "Just give me my clothes, Kaden. This really *isn't* a good idea."

But Kaden ignored her, was already stepping back and away, taking her clothes with him and leaving the fresh ones on the bed. She looked at them. Jeans and a delicate grey silk shirt. Rage filled her belly at being humiliated like this.

She indicated the clothes with a trembling hand. Too much emotion was coursing through her. More than she'd felt in years. "I won't wear your mistress's cast-offs. I'll walk out of here in this towel if I have to."

Kaden turned. He was silhouetted in the doorway, shoulders broad in a simple white shirt. Black trousers hugged his lean hips. Julia hadn't even noticed his still damp hair. She'd been so consumed by his overall presence.

He said, with a flash of fire in his eyes, "Be my guest, but there's really no need. Those clothes belong to Samia. You remember my younger sister? You're about the same size now. She's been living here for the last couple of years."

Immediately Julia felt petulant and exposed. She blushed. "Yes, I remember Samia." She'd always liked Kaden's next youngest sister, who had been bookish and painfully shy. Before she could say anything else, though, he was gone and the door had shut behind him.

Defeated, Julia contemplated the clothes. She took off the towel and put them on. There were even some knickers still in a plastic bag, and Julia could only figure that someone regularly stocked up Samia's wardrobe. The jeans were a little snug on her rear and thighs, and she felt extremely naked with no bra under the silk shirt. Her breasts weren't overly large, but they were too big for her to go bra-less and feel comfortable. There wasn't much she could do. It was either this or dress in the robe hanging off the back of the bathroom door. And she couldn't face Kaden in just a robe.

She went back into the bathroom and dried her hair

with the hairdryer. It dried a little frizzy, but there was not much she could do about that either. And, anyway, it wasn't as if she wanted to impress Kaden, was it? She scowled at the very thought.

Fresh resolve to insist on leaving fired her blood, and she picked up her shoes in one hand and took a deep breath before emerging from the suite, steeling herself to see Kaden again. When she did emerge though, it was to see him with his back to her at one of the main salon windows, looking out over the view. Something about his stance in that moment struck her as acutely lonely, but then he turned around and his sardonic visage made a mockery of her fanciful notion.

She hitched up her chin. "I'll get a taxi home. I can arrange to get my clothes from you another time."

Kaden's hand tightened reflexively on the glass he held. He should be saying *Yes, I'll call you a taxi.* He should be reminding himself that this was a very bad idea. But rational thought was very elusive as he looked at Julia.

Her hair drifted softly around her narrow shoulders. Like this, with the veneer of a successful, sophisticated woman stripped away, she might be nineteen again, and something inside him turned over. The grey silk shirt made the grey of her eyes look smoky and mysterious. He could remember thinking when he'd first met her that her eyes were a very icy light blue, but he had then realised that they were grey.

The silk shirt left little to the imagination. Her bare breasts pushed enticingly against the material, and under his gaze he could see her nipples harden to two thrusting points. His body responded forcibly. The jeans were too tight, but that only emphasized the curve of her hips and thighs. He wanted her to turn around so he could see her lush *derrière.* She'd always had a voluptuous bottom and generous breasts in contrast to her otherwise slender build.

Heat engulfed him, and he struggled for the first time in years to cling onto some control. Once again when it came to it…he couldn't let her go.

Julia was on fire under Kaden's very thorough inspection. "Please…" She wasn't even really aware of what she was saying, only that she wanted him to stop. "Don't look at me like that."

He smiled and went into seduction mode. "Like what? You're a beautiful woman, Julia. I'm sure you're used to having men's eyes on you."

Julia flushed at the slightly narrowed dark gaze, which hinted at steel underneath the apparent civility. The memory of what had happened just before she'd left Burquat flashed through her head and brought with it excoriating heat and guilt. And nausea… Kaden's eyes had been on her in her moment of humiliation. Even now she could remember the way that man had pulled her so close she'd felt as if she were suffocating, when all she'd wanted— She slammed the door on that memory.

She shook her head, "No, actually, I'm not. And this is not appropriate. I really should be leaving. So if you'll just call me a taxi…?"

Kaden smiled then, and it was the devil's smile. She sensed he'd come to some decision and it made her incredibly nervous.

"What's the rush? I'm sure you could do with a drink?"

Julia regarded this suddenly urbane pillar of solicitude suspiciously. Her shoes were unwieldy in her hand. She felt all at once awkward, hot, and yet pathetically reluctant to turn and never see Kaden again. That insidious yearning arose…the awareness that tonight was a bizarre coincidence. Fate. Surely the last time she would ever see him?

As much as she longed to get as far away as possible from this situation, and this man, a dangerous curiosity and a desire for him not to see how conflicted she was by this reunion made her shrug minutely and say grudgingly, "I suppose one drink wouldn't hurt. After all, it has been a long time."

He just looked at her. "Yes, it has." Hardly taking his eyes from hers, he indicated a bottle of cream liqueur on the sideboard and asked, "Do you still like this?"

Julia's belly swooped dangerously. He remembered her favourite drink? She'd only ever drunk it with him, and hadn't touched it in twelve years. She nodded dumbly and watched as his large, masculine yet graceful hands deftly poured the distinctive liquid. He replaced the bottle on the sideboard and then came and handed the delicately bulbous glass to Julia.

She took it, absurdly grateful that their fingers didn't touch. Bending her head, she took a sniff of the drink and then a quick sip, to disguise the flush she could feel rising when the smell precipitated a memory of drinking it with Kaden one magical night in his family's summer palace by the coast. It was the night they'd slept together for the first time.

For a second the full intensity of how much she'd loved him threatened to overwhelm her. And he'd casually poisoned those feelings and in one fell swoop destroyed her innocent idealism. Feeling tormented, and wondering if this avalanche of memories would ever go back into its box, she moved away from Kaden's tall, lean body, her eyes darting anywhere but to him.

She sensed him move behind her, and then he appeared in her peripheral vision.

"Please, won't you sit?"

So polite. As if nothing had happened. As if she hadn't given him her body, heart and soul.

Slamming another painful door in her mind, Julia said quickly, nervously, "Thank you."

She followed him, and when he sat on a plush couch, easily dominating it, she chose an armchair to the side, putting her shoes down beside her. She was as far away from him as she could get, legs together primly. She glanced at him to see a mocking look cross his face. She didn't care. This new Kaden intimidated her. There was nothing of the boy she'd known. They'd both just been teenagers after all...until he'd had to grow up overnight, after the death of his father.

Now he was a man—infinitely more commanding. She'd seen a glimpse of this more formidable Kaden the last time they'd spoken in Burquat, but that had been a mere precursor of the powerful man opposite her now.

Julia felt exposed in her bare feet and the flimsy shirt. It was too silky against her bare flesh. Her nipples were hard, tingling. She hadn't felt this effortlessly aroused once during her marriage, or since she'd been with Kaden, and the realisation made her feel even more exposed. She struggled to hang on to the fact that she was a successful and relatively sophisticated woman. She'd been married and divorced. She was no naïve virgin any more. She could handle this. She had to remember that, while he had devastated *her*, he'd been untouched after their relationship ended. She'd never forget how emotionless he'd been when they said goodbye. It was carved into her soul.

Remembering who the clothes belonged to gave her a moment of divine inspiration. With forced brightness she asked, "How *is* Samia? She must be at least twenty-four by now?"

Kaden observed Julia from under hooded lids. He was in no hurry to answer her question or engage in small talk. It was more than disconcerting how *right* it felt to have her here. And even more so to acknowledge that the vaguely unsettled feeling he'd been experiencing for what felt like years was dissipating.

She intrigued him more than he cared to admit. He might have imagined that by now she would be far more polished, would have cultivated the hard veneer he was used to in the kind of women he socialised with.

Curbing the urge to stand and pace out the intense conflict inside him as her vulnerability tugged at his jaded emotions, Kaden struggled to remain sitting and remember what she'd asked.

"Samia? She's twenty-five, and she's getting married at the end of this week. To the Sultan of Al-Omar. She's in B'harani for the preparations right now."

Julia's eyes widened, increasing Kaden's levels of inner tension and desire. He cursed silently. He couldn't stand up now even if he wanted to—not if he didn't want her to see exactly the effect she had on him. He vacillated between intense anger at himself for bringing her here at all, and the assertion that she would not be walking out through his front door any time soon.

Kaden was used to clear, concise thinking—not this churning maelstrom. It was too reminiscent of what had happened before. And yet even as he thought that the tantalising prospect came into his mind: why not take her again? Tonight? Why not exorcise this desire which mocked him with its presence?

"The Sultan of Al-Omar?" Julia shook her head, not liking the speculative gleam in Kaden's eyes. Blonde hair slipped over her shoulders. She tried to focus on stringing a sentence together. "Samia was so painfully shy. It must be difficult for her to take on such a public role?"

An irrational burst of guilt rushed through Kaden. He'd seen Samia recently, here in London before she'd left, and had felt somewhat reassured by her stoic calm in the face of her impending nuptials. But Julia was reminding him what a challenge this would be for his naturally introverted sister. And he was surprised that Julia remembered such a detail.

It made his voice harsh. "Samia is a woman now, with responsibilities to her country and her people. A marriage with Sultan Sadiq benefits both our countries."

"So it is an arranged marriage, then?"

Kaden nodded his head, not sure where the defensiveness he was feeling stemmed from. "Of course—just as my own marriage was arranged and just as my next marriage will be arranged." He quirked a brow. "I presume your marriage was a love match, and yet you did not fare any better if you too are divorced?"

Julia hid the dart of emotion at hearing him say he would marry again and avoided his eye. Had her marriage been a love match? In general terms, yes—it had. After all, she and John had married willingly, with no pressure on either side. But she knew in her heart of hearts that she hadn't truly loved John. And he'd known it too.

Something curdled in her belly at having to justify herself to this man who had haunted her for so long. She looked back at him as steadily as she could. "No, we didn't fare any better. However, I know plenty of arranged marriages work out very well, so I wish Samia all the best."

"Children?"

For a moment Julia didn't catch what Kaden had said it had been uttered so curtly. "Children?" she repeated, and he nodded.

Julia felt another kind of pain lance her. The memory of the look of shame on her husband's face, the way he had closed in on himself and started to retreat, which had marked the beginning of the end of their marriage.

She shook her head and said, a little defiantly, "Of course not. Do you think I would be here if I had?" And then she cursed herself inwardly. She didn't want Kaden analysing why she *had* come. "My husband—*ex*-husband—couldn't… We had difficulties… And you? Did you have children?"

That slightly mocking look crossed his face again, because she must know well that his status as a childless divorcee was common knowledge. But he just shook his head. "No, no children."

His mouth had become a bitter line, and Julia shivered minutely because it reminded her of how he'd morphed within days from an ardent lover into a cold stranger.

"My ex-wife's mother suffered a horrific and near-fatal childbirth and stuffed my wife's head with tales of horror and pain. As a result Amira developed a phobia about childbirth. It was so strong that when she did discover she was pregnant she went without my knowledge to get a termination. Soon afterwards I started proceedings to divorce."

Julia gave an audible gasp and Kaden saw her eyes grow wide. He knew how it sounded—so stark. His jaw was tight with tension. How on earth had he let those words spill so blithely from his mouth? He'd just told Julia something that only a handful of people knew. The secret of his ex-wife's actions was something he discussed with nobody. As were the painstaking efforts he'd made to help her overcome that fear after the abortion. But to no avail. Eventually it had been his wife who had insisted they divorce, knowing that she could never give him an heir. She hadn't been prepared to confront her fears.

Kaden's somewhat brutal dismissal of a wife who hadn't been able to perform her duty made a shiver run through Julia. The man she'd known had been compassionate, idealistic.

To divert attention away from the dismay she felt at recognising just how much he'd changed, she said quickly, "I thought divorce was illegal in Burquat?"

Kaden took a measured sip of his amber-coloured drink. "It used to be. Things have changed a lot since you were there. It's been slow but steady reform, undoing the more conservative laws of my father and his forebears."

A rush of tenderness took Julia by surprise, coming so soon after her feeling repelled by his treatment of his wife. Kaden had always been so passionate about reform for his country, and now he was doing it.

Terrified that he would see something of that emotion rising up within her, Julia stood up jerkily and walked over to the window, clutching her glass in her hand.

She took in the view. Kaden had told her about this apartment, right in the centre of London. Pain, bitter-sweet, rushed through her. He had once mentioned that she should move in here when she returned to college in London—so that he could make sure she was protected, and so she would be waiting for him when he came over. But those words had all been part of his seductive patter. Meaningless. A wave of sadness gripped her.

She didn't hear Kaden move, and jumped when his deep voice came from her right, far too close. "Why did you divorce your husband, Julia?"

Because I never loved him the way I loved you. The words reverberated around her head. Never in a million years had she imagined she would be standing in a room listening to Kaden ask her that question.

Eventually, when she felt as if she had some measure of control, she glanced at him. He was standing with one shoulder propped nonchalantly against the wall, looking at her from under hooded lids. With one hand in his pocket, the glass held loosely in the other, he could have stepped straight out of a fashion magazine.

He looked dark and dangerous, and Julia gulped—because she felt that sense of danger reverberate within her and ignite a fire. She tried to ignore the sensation, telling herself it was overactive hormones mixed in with too many evocative memories and the loaded situation they were now in. She looked back out of the window with an effort. She felt hot and tingly all over, her belly heavy with desire.

"I…we just grew apart." She shook her head. "It seemed like a good idea, but it never really worked. And our difficulty with having children was the last straw. There wasn't enough to keep us together. I'm glad there were no children. It wouldn't have been the right environment to bring them into."

Julia had never told Kaden that she was adopted, or about her own visceral feelings on the subject of having children. She'd never told anyone. It was too bound up in painful emotions for her. And perhaps she hadn't told him for a reason—because on some level she'd been afraid of his judgement, and that what they shared hadn't been real. She'd been right to be afraid.

She was aware of tension emanating from Kaden and didn't want to look at him, afraid he might see the emotion she felt she couldn't hide. Her face always gave her away. He was the one who had told her that as he'd held her face in his hands one day…

Suddenly from out of the still ominously cloudy sky came a jagged flash of lightning. Julia jumped so violently that liquid sloshed out of her glass. Immediately shocked and embarrassed by her overreaction, she stepped back. "I'm sorry…"

Kaden was there in an instant. He took the glass out of her hand, placing it down on the table alongside his own. He was back in front of her before she could steel herself not to react. His dark eyes looked her up and down and then rested on her chest. As if mesmerised, Julia followed his gaze to see where some of the drink had landed on her shirt, right over one breast, and now the material was clinging to the rounded slope.

Panicky, Julia stepped back, "I'll get a cloth… I don't want Samia's shirt to get ruined."

A big hand snaked out and caught her upper arm. "Leave it."

Kaden's voice was unbearably harsh, and in that instant the air between became even heavier and more charged. As if the tension and atmosphere between them was directly affecting the weather, a huge booming roll of thunder sounded outside.

Julia flinched, eyes glued to Kaden's with some kind of sick fascination. Faintly she said, "I thought the storm was over."

With a move so smooth she didn't even feel it happening Kaden put his hands on her arms and pulled her closer. Their bodies were almost touching.

"I think the storm is just beginning."

For a second confusion made Julia's head foggy. She didn't seem to be able to separate out his words, or even understand what Kaden was saying. And then she realised, when she saw how hot his gaze had become and how it moved down to her mouth. Desire was stamped onto the stark lines of his face and Julia's heart beat fast in response. Because it was a look that had haunted her dreams for ever.

Desperately trying to fight the urge to succumb to the waves of need beating through her veins, she shook her head and tensed, trying to pull back out of Kaden's grip. His hands just tightened.

"Kaden, *no*. I shouldn't be here…we shouldn't have met again."

"But we did meet. And you're here now."

Julia asserted stiffly, "I didn't agree to come here for this."

Kaden shook his head, and a tiny harsh smile touched his mouth. "From the moment we stood in front of each other in that room earlier the possibility of *this* has existed."

Bitterness rang in Julia's voice. "Even when you pretended not to know me?"

More lightning flashed outside, quickly followed by the roll of thunder. The unmistakable sound of torrential rain started to lash against the window.

"Even then."

Nothing seemed to be throwing Kaden off. Had he somehow magically dimmed the lights in the room? Julia wondered frantically, feeling as though reality was slipping out of her grasp. The past was meshing into the present, and the future was fast becoming irrelevant.

Julia tried again. "The possibility of this stopped existing twelve years ago in Burquat—or have you forgotten when you informed me our *affair* was past its sell-by date?" Bitterness laced her voice, but she couldn't pretend it wasn't there, much as she would have loved to feign insouciance. The rawness of that day was vivid.

Kaden's hands were steady. "I don't wish to discuss the past, Julia. The past bears no relationship to this moment."

"How can you say that? The past is the reason I'm standing here now."

Kaden shook his head, eyes glowing with dark embers, effortlessly stoking Julia's desire higher and higher, despite what her head might be saying.

"I would have wanted you even if tonight was the first time we'd met."

His flattery did nothing for Julia's ego. The evidence of how unmoved he was by the past broke something apart inside her. Of course it had no effect on him now. Because he felt nothing for her—just as he'd never really felt anything for her.

Julia tensed as much as she could. She had to get out of there. Things were spiralling out of all control. "Well, the past might not be relevant to you, but it is to me, and I think this is a very bad idea."

Kaden's eyes flashed, showing Julia a glimpse of the emotion that thickened the atmosphere between them, no matter how he might deny it. "*This* is desire, pure and simple. We're two single consenting adults and I want you."

Julia looked up, helpless to pull away or articulate any kind of sane response. Which should be *no*. How was it possible that this desire hadn't abated one bit? That if anything it felt stronger? There were so many layers of meaning here, and Kaden wanted to ignore all of that. As if they had never met before.

He lifted a hand and slid it around the back of her neck, under the fall of her hair, and pulled her even closer. Huskily he said, "I didn't expect this. I didn't expect that if I ever saw you again I would feel this way. Perhaps this was meant to be…a chance encounter to burn ourselves free of this insatiable desire."

Insatiable desire. That was exactly how it felt—how it had always felt between them. Moments after making love Julia had always been ashamed of how quickly she'd craved Kaden's touch again, and only the fact that it had been mutual had stopped her shame from overwhelming her.

As he said, he hadn't expected to see her again. And she could well believe that he'd not expected to desire her again. But he did, and obviously resented it. Why wouldn't he? He'd turned his back on her, and he'd bedded plenty of women far more beautiful than Julia since then. It must be galling to meet your first lover and realise you still wanted her. That made Julia feel acutely vulnerable. But it was too late.

Kaden had pulled her even closer, and now her soft belly touched his hard-muscled form—far harder than she remembered—and his head was lowering to hers. She tried to stiffen, to register her rejection, but everything was blocked out when she felt the explosive touch of Kaden's mouth to hers. Did it coincide with another clap of thunder outside or was that in her head?

Her heart spasmed in her chest, as if given an electric shock, and as his mouth moved and fitted to hers like a missing jigsaw piece she fell down into a dark vortex of desire so intense that it obliterated any kind of rational thought. Her hands had gone automatically to his chest, but instead of pushing him away they clung. The feel of powerful muscles under his shirt was intoxicating.

Time stood still. Everything stood still except for their two hearts, beating fast. Blood was rushing through veins and arteries, pumping to parts of Julia's body that hadn't been stimulated in a long, long time.

Kaden was seduction incarnate. His hands moved over and down her back, cupping her bottom in the tight jeans, floating sensuously over the silk shirt. With an easy expertise he certainly hadn't displayed when she'd known him before he coaxed her mouth open and his tongue stroked along hers, making a faint mewl come from the back of her throat.

Through the heat haze in her head and her body Julia felt something urgent trying to get through to her. Kaden's touch was all at once achingly familiar, and yet so different from how she remembered. They'd been so young, and their passion had been raw and untutored. The man who held her in his arms now was not raw and untutored. He was a consummate seducer, well-practised in the art. His body was different too. Muscles were filled out and harder.

It was that realisation that finally broke the spell cast around Julia. Plus the fact that within a mere hour of meeting Kaden again she was kissing him like a sex-starved groupie.

Wrenching herself away in one abruptly violent move, Julia staggered backwards, looking at Kaden's flushed face and glittering eyes. "I don't know you. You're a stranger to me now. I don't do this… I don't make love to strangers."

Something dark crossed Kaden's handsome features. He drawled, "From what I recall, you found it remarkably easy to make love to relative strangers."

With the memory of that incident so vivid, Julia lashed out. "It was just a kiss, Kaden. A stupid kiss. It meant nothing… It was just—" She stopped abruptly. Had she really been about to blurt out that she'd only allowed that man to kiss her because she'd felt so desperately insecure after days of silence from Kaden? That she'd pathetically wanted to try and prove to herself that his touch alone couldn't be the only touch she'd ever crave?

She clamped her mouth shut, burning inside. This man would never know that her experiment had backfired spectacularly—on more levels than one.

She had to claw back some sense of sanity. Some sense of the independent woman she'd become. Her voice was shaky. "This is not a good idea, Kaden. The past is the past and we should not be revisiting it."

Kaden felt tight and hot inside. With ruthless effort he excised the image of her kissing that man from his mind. What on earth had prompted him to bring up that kiss?

The last thing he wanted was for Julia to know that he remembered the incident. And yet it was like the stain of a tattoo on his memory, the jealousy fresh.

She was avoiding Kaden's eye. He might have appreciated the dark humour of the situation if he'd been in a better mood: merely *kissing* her just now had had a more explosive effect on his libido than anything he'd shared with a woman in years. If ever. Her chest was rising and falling rapidly. Some more buttons had opened on her shirt, exposing the shadowy line of her cleavage, and his erection just got harder. If that was possible.

The fact that what she said was right irked him beyond belief. He knew with a soul-deep certainly that to explore this desire with *this* woman had danger written all over it. He had a sense of having escaped the fire years before, only to be standing right on its edge again.

But stronger than that was this life-force rushing through his veins, along with the very carnal urge to sate himself. It was heady, and it made him feel as if he was awakening from a long sleep. He could no more turn back from it than he could stop breathing. He struggled to control himself. The rawness of what he was feeling was rising up, and Kaden ruthlessly drove it down, back to depths he'd never plumbed and had no intention of doing so now.

He crossed the room to where Julia stood. She looked up. Those grey eyes were dark and troubled. A line of pink slashed each cheek, and her lips were full and tender-looking. In a completely instinctive gesture he reached out and tucked some hair behind her ear, only realising as he did it that he'd used to do that all the time. His jaw clenching hard was the only sign that he'd recognised this tell-tale gesture which was at such odds with the dark emotion seething through his gut. *Jealousy.* He had to distance himself from their past, focus on the present.

"If we had met at any other time we wouldn't have been available, and yet this desire would still have blown up. It would have made a mockery of the fact that twelve years had gone by. And of our marriages." He went on, his deep voice mesmerising, "But we're both free and single now, two consenting adults."

Julia knew she should run—and fast. Get away and pray to God that she never saw Kaden again. But her feet wouldn't move. The way he'd casually reached out to tuck her hair behind her ear had broken something apart inside her, bringing with it an onslaught of memories of so many moments when he'd done that. It had been the first physical gesture he'd made to her.

Fatefully, knowing that on some level she was making a momentous decision by *not* leaving, Julia couldn't seem to turn away. She felt curiously lethargic—as if she'd been running towards something for a long time, only to have finally reached her destination. She wanted this man with a hunger she'd known only once before… for *him.*

She'd fully expected that if they ever met again that he would act as dismissively as he had earlier…and yet here she was. He wasn't pretending not to know her now. He was looking at her as if she was the only woman on the planet. That elusive feeling of home and connection that she'd only ever found with him whispered to her like a siren song, calling her to seek it again.

Desperately she fought it—going that way again could only end in worse devastation. Clinging furiously to some last vestige of pride, to the illusion that she had control, she backed away. "Just because we've met again, it doesn't mean anything, Kaden. It doesn't mean that we have to end up…in bed."

For a long tense moment they just looked at each other, and then, after another ear-splitting crack of thunder, the electricity went off.

Julia gasped and Kaden cursed. "The storm must have outed the power. Wait here. I'll get some candles."

Julia felt Kaden move away from her and took a deep, shaky breath. The darkness seemed to envelop her in a cloak of collusion. It made her want to forget the outside world, forget to remember their history. To give in to what he was offering. She wanted him so badly she shook.

Desperately she tried to remember the awful excoriating pain of the moment when he'd coolly informed her that all they'd shared had been a summer fling, that he had a life of responsibilities that didn't include her. But it was like trying to hold onto a wispy cloud. All she knew was the exhilaration rushing through her blood, the heightened awareness of desire.

Through the silence of the apartment she heard a crash somewhere and a colourful curse. They were sounds that *should* have been restoring her sanity, making her more determined to leave. But instead they were only firing her desire. She heard a movement and saw flickering light. This was it.

Kaden came back into the room, and in the soft glow Julia could only look at him and marvel at the shadows which made his face seem even more mysterious, his eyes two dark pools. He put down the candle and came closer and closer, until his body was just inches away from hers. His heat enveloped her, along with his exotic masculine scent. It made her think of hot nights in the desert, and of even hotter things.

"Julia, I don't want to analyse why this has happened like this. I don't want to discuss the past… I just want you."

She looked up at Kaden. So many feelings were rushing through her like a torrent, but one above all others. She wanted him too. She'd dreamt for years of seeing him again. He'd cast her out without a moment's hesitation, and when she'd heard about his nuptials something in her had died. So she had given in and accepted John's proposal, believing it was futile to love a ghost.

But he wasn't a ghost any more. He was flesh and blood and standing right in front of her. And then he reached out a hand and cupped her jaw, his thumb stroking her cheek. She was undone. When he pulled her closer she didn't resist. Because she couldn't.

CHAPTER FOUR

KADEN found himself relishing the other-worldliness that enforced darkness imposed, surrounding them in this cocoon. Julia's eyes were huge, her breaths coming short and rapid, and as he lowered his head so that his mouth could drink from hers he felt an inalienable sense of rightness. It was too strong to deny or question or rail against. His mouth settled over Julia's, his arms pulled her close, and when he felt her breasts crushed against his chest he was lost.

The outside world—the lashing rain against the windows and the intermittent thunder and lightning—all faded into the background as flames of heat started licking around them.

After what seemed like an aeon had passed Kaden pulled back. Julia was stunned, her limbs jelly-like. Her mouth felt swollen and her heart was hammering as if she'd just run half a marathon. Her hands were around Kaden's neck, his breath was harsh, and she could feel the hard ridge of his erection against her belly.

He just said coarsely, "Julia."

She didn't stop him when he shifted slightly so that he could pick her up into his arms. "Take the candle," he instructed roughly.

Half in a daze, Julia looked down to see the flickering candle on a table. She reached down to pick it up in its stand and then Kaden was striding out of the room, the soft light guiding their way to a door which he all but kicked open. In the shadowy half-light Julia could pick out a huge bed and unmistakably masculine furnishings. Kaden's bedroom.

A sliver of sanity returned, and Kaden must have felt her tense, because he looked down into her face and said implacably, "There is no going back from here."

Her breath was suspended for a long moment, and then the enormity of meeting Kaden again struck home. How fleeting this night would be. The weight of her yearning for this man was heavy on her shoulders, and it was too strong to deny, much as the tiny sliver of sanity she had left might be urging her to. Slowly. Fatefully, she shook her head. "I don't want to go back."

He carried her over to the chest of drawers, where she put down the candle, then let her slide down his body, his hands touching her from shoulder to waist to hip. He pushed some of her hair back over one shoulder and bent his head to her neck, pressing a kiss there. Julia's head fell back. It was too heavy to hold up. Her blood was hot as it pumped through her veins.

Kaden's fingers came to her shirt and he started to undo the buttons in the slippery fabric. She shivered slightly when the air whispered over her bare skin. Soon her shirt hung open. Kaden drew back and stood to his full height.

He was downright intimidating in the dusky light, with no help from an obscured moon, but he was also *thrilling*. He was a big man all over. Julia watched with a drying mouth as he coolly started to open his own buttons. Part of her wanted to be as bold as she'd once been and brush his hands aside so that she could do it. But this wasn't the past. She was more cautious now, no matter how time seemed to be blurring here tonight.

His shirt was open, and with an economy of movement he pulled it off, revealing his awe-inspiring chest. It was broad and tautly muscled, and he had filled out since she'd seen him last. Coarse dark hair covered his pectorals, leading downwards in a dark line to just above his belt.

A finger to her chin lifted her face back up and Julia flamed guiltily. She'd all but been licking her lips at the prospect of seeing him fully naked for the first time in years.

Instead of pushing her shirt off her shoulders and arms, Kaden's big hands came to her waist, spanning it easily. His action pushed the shirt off her breasts, revealing them to his incendiary gaze. She could see a pulse throb in his neck and her belly quivered. Hot, wet heat moistened her sex in readiness.

Kaden breathed out. "So beautiful…you're so damn beautiful."

He cupped one fleshy weight in his hand and a thumb moved back and forth rhythmically over the tight peak. Julia moaned, and didn't even realise she was pushing her breast into his hand to increase the friction.

With a languorous movement he brought his thumb to his mouth and sucked it deep, before moving it back and repeating the action, moistening the hard tip. Julia moaned even louder, her breath coming short and fast. Excitement was building, ratcheting her inner tension upwards.

"Kaden…please."

"Please what?" he asked, almost casually. "Do you want me to put my mouth on you? Do you want me to taste you?"

Julia was almost weeping. "Yes…"

Kaden's head came down and his mouth closed unerringly over her already deeply sensitised nipple. Silky hair brushed the hot skin of her breast, adding to the exquisite sensation. He sucked so hard that Julia cried out, her fingers arrowing through his hair, holding him in place. His other hand was moulding and cupping the flesh of her other breast, readying it too for his ministrations.

His mouth moved to the second peak and Julia's legs all but buckled. Ruthlessly, with an arm around her waist, Kaden clamped her to him, not letting her fall, all the while subjecting her to something on the knife-edge of pleasure and pain.

Julia was fast losing sight of any reality. She was made up of sensations, a slave to this man and his touch. He was so much more confident than she remembered. He knew exactly what to do, where she ached to be touched.

As abruptly as he'd started torturing her with his mouth he stood back again, and with his hands clamped on her waist he drew her into him with an urgency that sent blood rushing to her pelvis. His head bent, mouth finding hers, tongue delving deep and seeking hers. The friction of her sensitised breasts against his chest was delicious torture. Through the haze of desire and excitement Julia felt a wild surge of exhilaration at being with this man again. It was as if now she'd given in to it she could fully appreciate the experience.

Blindly obeying the deep call of her blood, Julia let

her hands seek and fumble with Kaden's belt and zip, undoing them with a feverish intensity. While their mouths still clung, Julia pushed his trousers down over his lean hips. She could feel Kaden step out of them and kick them away. And then her hands were on his boxers.

He drew back at that, and she could see his eyes glittering. Her breasts were heavy. Her blood was on fire. Not taking her eyes off his, she put her fingers between his hot skin and the material and pulled them down. It was only when they snagged that she looked. The bulge of his erection was formidable. Running a finger around the rim of his boxers, unaware of the look of torture on Kaden's face, Julia stopped just where she could feel the smooth head of him.

Slowly she pulled the boxers out, free of his erection, and then they too were slid down over his powerfully muscled thighs. It reminded Julia again of the national sport that Kaden so loved to play, which had broken his nose at least once. It had looked barbaric to her: men stripped to the waist, using a crude form of shortened hockey stick to whack a ball between two goals. Part of the play was to crash into one another and divert each other from the ball. It was visceral, exciting and undeniably violent. And Kaden excelled at it.

But now she couldn't take her eyes off his impressive erection, springing free from the cradle of black hair. Moisture beaded the tip enticingly, and she could feel her own body moisten in answer.

His voice broke the spell. "I'm feeling a little underdressed here."

Julia's wide gaze clashed with his as he pushed her shirt off her shoulders, down her arms, from where it slithered to the floor in a pool of grey silk. Then his efficient hands were on her jeans, flicking open the button and pulling down the zip. Julia barely had a chance to get her breath before she felt him tugging them down over her hips and thighs.

Any embarrassment because the jeans were too small was lost when she saw how his gaze roved hungrily over her body. She sucked in a shaky breath when he took her by the hand to lead her to the bed. The candlelight and the dark, ominous sky outside made everything seem even more unreal. But the heat between her and Kaden was very real.

As he pushed her back onto the bed she realised with an illicit thrill that his touch was all at once familiar and yet that of a stranger. He was truly a man now, and she sensed a hunger in him that hadn't been there before, an easy dominance.

He joined her on the cool sheets and all rational thought fled. Pulling her into his body, touching her chest to chest and down, he kissed her again, deeply, as if he couldn't get enough of kissing her. Julia sank back into the covers, relishing the latent strength in Kaden's powerful form. His hand smoothed its way down, over her chest and to her belly. Fingers seeking even further until they encountered her pants.

With a perfunctory movement they were dispatched, and Kaden pushed her thighs apart, his hand seeking between her legs to where her body told of its readiness for him.

One finger stroked in and out of her moist heat. Julia's hands gripped Kaden's shoulders. She couldn't breathe, and almost arched off the bed when one finger was joined by another one, opening her up, stretching her, preparing her for his own body. Julia's hand sought his erection and wrapped around it, squeezing and moving up and down—a silent plea for him to stop torturing her. She couldn't speak, couldn't articulate anything.

Kaden shifted and was moving down her body, pressing kisses along her belly until his mouth was at the juncture of her legs and his tongue was tasting her as he'd once shocked her by doing all those years ago. She gasped, but ruthlessly he held her thighs wide apart, baring her to his mouth and that wickedly stabbing tongue.

He reached one hand up to find her breast and rolled a nipple between his fingers. Without anything to cling onto, Julia felt her body tighten in a spasm of pleasure so intense she didn't even notice when Kaden moved again, so that his huge body now lay between her legs.

Shattered from the intensity of the strongest orgasm she could remember having, she could only lie there in a stupor as Kaden took himself in his hand and stroked the head of his erection back and forth against her moistened sex. Her body was already greedy for him, her muscles still clenching as if trying to suck him in. At some point he'd had the sense to don protection, and Julia was exceedingly grateful—because all concerns for practicalities had gone out of the window.

Torturously he let himself be sucked in slowly, sheathing the head in her heat before pulling out. Julia moaned softly, her eyes glued to Kaden's harsh face. He looked so stark, like a pagan god stripped bare of all civility. And then he leaned over her on both hands and with one cataclysmic thrust seated himself in her fully. All the way to the hilt. Julia gasped at his size, but the fleeting pain quickly morphed to an intense pleasure, as if her body recognised him and was rejoicing.

"You…" he said roughly. "You are the only one who has ever made me feel like this…"

Julia asked brokenly, "Like what?"

"Like I'm not even human any more."

And with that he started up a remorseless rhythm, stroking in and out, his thrusts so long and full that Julia pulled up her legs to allow him to slide even deeper. There had not been one second of hesitation on her part in allowing him into her body. It had taken her husband months to woo her, for her to trust him enough to sleep with him. She'd still been so shaken by what had happened in Burquat… But here with Kaden it felt so natural and right she couldn't fight it.

The tremors of her last orgasm were still dying away as new tremors started up, even more intense than the last time. Sweat beaded her brow and dampened her skin. And Kaden still moved between her legs and inside her, as if he wanted to wring out this pleasure for as long as possible. Julia knew she wouldn't last. Head flung back, she arched upwards and splintered all over again, just as Kaden's thrusts increased, and when the storm in her body abated he gave a guttural groan and sank over her, his huge body stilling.

During the night Julia woke briefly to see that the storm had finally died away. The candle had gone out and she was tucked against Kaden's chest, his arms tight around her like a vice. The moon peeked out from behind a cloud.

The storm outside might have abated, but another storm was starting up inside her.

What on earth had she done?

Her thoughts must have made her tense, because she

could feel Kaden stirring behind her. He shifted them so that she lay on her back, looking up into slumbrous long-lashed eyes. She felt extremely vulnerable. She'd never expected to see him again, much less—

"Kaden… I—"

But he cut her off by putting a finger over her mouth. He shook his head, a lock of silky black hair flopping over his forehead, making him look sexily dishevelled. "Don't say a word. I don't want to hear it."

He took her mouth with his, and within seconds the conflagration that had burnt them before was starting up again. Julia's mind was screaming at her to stop, but the call of her blood was too strong. Kaden didn't even move over her this time. He gently shifted her so that she was on her side and lifted up one of her legs, pulling it back over his thigh. She gasped out loud when she felt him surge up and into her from behind, his arm snaking around her midriff and holding her firm as he thrust upwards.

His other hand cupped a breast, trapping a nipple between his fingers, and Julia helplessly fell into the fire all over again.

When Julia woke next she knew it was morning. She could sense the bright sunlight on her face. She was replete and lethargic. And at peace. *At peace?* The words resounded in her head as she registered her nakedness and the pleasurable ache throughout her body.

Almost superstitiously, she didn't open her eyes. She didn't need to; the pictures forming behind her closed lids were too lurid. Images formed into a set of scenarios: seeing Kaden at the top of the stairs after he'd been announced at the club; standing in front of him and regstering that sardonic coolness; the rain; coming back here; the lights going out…and then heat. Nothing but heat. Maybe it had all been a dream. God only knew she'd had a few like it…

"I can tell that you're going through exactly what I went through when I woke. And, yes, every second of it happened for real." The voice was dry, mocking, and not a dream.

Julia's eyes flew open and she squinted in the bright light. Mercifully the sheet was up over her breasts. She pulled it up higher and could see Kaden now, standing at the window, looking gorgeous and pristine in a dark suit, drinking nonchalantly from what looked like an espresso cup.

He gestured with his other hand to a small breakfast table. "There's coffee there for you too, and some orange juice and a croissant."

Her stomach churned. It was excruciating to be facing Kaden like this. She'd been so *easy*. She came up on one arm and bit her lip, looked down. Her eyes were watering, and she couldn't tell if it was from the bright sunlight or looking at Kaden. The storm from last night had well and truly passed, and already the bitter recrimination was starting.

What on earth had she been thinking? Had one thunderstorm rewired her entire brain?

He moved forward then, and put down his cup. He came closer to the bed. Julia sat up awkwardly. Kaden's eyes were very black and intense on her, and already she could feel the heat of renewed desire deep within her.

"I'm here until the end of the week, when I have to fly to Al-Omar for Samia's wedding. I'd like to see you again, Julia."

Julia didn't know what to make of the maelstrom that erupted inside her at his words. She'd been expecting him to tell her casually to let herself out of the apartment when she was ready. "You want to see me again?"

He shrugged, oozing insouciance and an ease with this morning after situation. Another indication of the urbane seducer he'd become. "I don't see why not. I think we have unfinished business…why not finish it?"

Julia's mouth twisted. "You mean have an affair for a few days and then walk away?"

His mouth thinned. "It doesn't have to be as crass as that. You can't deny the attraction is as strong as ever. Why not indulge it to its natural conclusion? I don't see it lasting for longer than a few days."

That warm spread of desire suddenly cooled. Julia sat up straighter, pulling the sheet around her carefully. She felt seriously dishevelled and at a disadvantage in front of Kaden like this. She attempted her haughtiest look. "I'm extremely busy this week. I don't know if I have time to fit in an…*affair*."

Kaden's face became mocking. "I don't plan on spending the *days* with you, Julia, I was thinking more along the lines of the evenings…and the nights."

Instantly she castigated herself. Of course he wasn't talking about having *conversations*. She stood up, clinging onto the sheet like a lifeline.

"It's a crazy idea, Kaden. Last night was…" She bit her lip. "It should never have happened."

He strolled closer, and Julia would have moved back if she could—but the bed was at the back of her legs. Up close to him in her bare feet, she was reminded of how huge he was—and how utterly gorgeous. Once again the juxtaposition between the boy and the man was overwhelming. But his hands were shoved deep in his pockets, and she sensed an underlying tension to his otherwise suave manner.

He took one hand out then, and touched his knuckles to her chin. She gritted her jaw against his touch. His dark eyes roved her face and she couldn't make out any emotion. It made her wonder at the depths this civility hid from her.

Steel ran through his voice, impacting her. "Well, it did happen, Julia. And it's going to happen again. I'll pick you up from your house this evening at seven."

And with that he stepped back and strolled away.

Julia's mouth opened and closed ineffectually. She couldn't get over his easy arrogance that she would just fall in with his wishes. "You..." she spluttered. "You can't just seriously think that I will—"

He turned at the door. "I don't think, Julia. I *know*." He arched a brow. "I believe you said you were busy this week? You'd better get a move on. You'll find your clothes hanging in the closet. Help yourself to whatever you need. One of my cars will be waiting outside. You will be taken wherever you wish to go."

Kaden turned and left the room, shutting the door behind him. He didn't like the way he'd just had to battle to control himself enough not to topple Julia back onto that bed and take her again. And again. She'd looked tousled and thoroughly bedded, and far too reminiscent of memories he'd long suppressed. And he was *still* ignoring the voice in his head urging him to walk away, to forget he'd seen her again. He *should* have been able to leave last night as a one-off, an aberration. But he couldn't do it.

He was well aware that he'd just acted like some medieval autocrat, but the truth was he hadn't wanted to give her a chance to argue with him. To have her tell him that she was refusing to see him again, or point out again that this shouldn't have happened. He might have appreciated the fact that this was the first time a woman was clearly less than eager to share his bed if he'd been able to think past the urgent lust he still felt.

Standing in front of Julia just now, he'd not been able to think beyond the immediate future. He'd had a vision of being in London for the next few days, and the thought of not seeing her again had been repugnant.

He tried to rationalise it now. Their desire was clearly far from sated, but he had no doubt a couple of nights would be more than enough to rid himself of this bizarre need to reconnect with an ex-lover. *An ex-lover who almost had you in such thrall that you forgot what your priorities were.*

Kaden scowled, but didn't stop. By the time he reached his waiting car his face was as dark as thunder, tension vibrating off him in waves.

Minutes later Julia was still standing looking at the closed door, clutching the rumpled sheet, her mouth half open. And to her utter chagrin she couldn't drum up anything other than intense excitement at the thought of seeing Kaden again. Even after he'd so arrogantly informed her that it would suit him to have an affair while he was in London, to fill his time. Pathetic.

Last night ran through her brain like a bad movie, and all she could remember was the wanton way she'd succumbed to his caresses over and over again. The way she'd sought him out, her hand wrapping around him, eager to seduce him.

She groaned out loud and finally stumbled towards the bathroom. That was nearly worse. His scent was heavy in the air, steam still evident from his recent shower. She could see that glorious body in her mind's eye—naked, with water sluicing down over taut, hard muscles and contours.

She tore off the sheet and turned on the shower, relishing the hot pounding spray, but try as she might she couldn't stop older memories flooding her brain, superseding the more recent and humiliating ones. Pandora's Box had been well and truly opened. All she could think of now were the awful last weeks and days in Burquat. Even under the hot spray, Julia shivered.

A few weeks before she'd been due to return to England to complete her studies, Julia and Kaden had returned from a trip to the desert where they'd celebrated her birthday. She'd been so in love with him, and she'd believed that he'd loved her too. He'd *told* her he loved her. So why wouldn't she have believed him?

But, as clear as if it was yesterday, she could remember watching him walk away from her when they got back to Burquat. For some reason she'd superstitiously wished for him to turn around and smile at her, but he hadn't. That image of his tall, rangy body walking away from her had proved to be an ominous sign. She'd not seen him again until shortly before she was due to leave Burquat.

That very night it had been announced that the Emir wasn't well, and so Kaden had in effect become acting ruler. Heartsore for Kaden, because she'd known he was close to his father even though he'd been a somewhat distant figure, she'd made attempts to see him. But she'd been turned back time and time again by stern-looking aides.

It was as if he'd been spirited away. Days had passed, Julia had made preparations to go home and there had still been no sign or word from Kaden. She'd put it down to his father's frailty and the huge responsibility he faced as the incumbent ruler. She'd never realised until then how different it would have been if he had already been ruler. Much to her shame, she hadn't been able to stop the feeling of insecurity growing when there was no word, even though she'd known it was selfish.

A few nights before she'd been due to leave, Julia had given in to the urging of some fellow archaeology students and gone out for a drink, telling herself it was futile to waste another evening pining for Kaden. She hadn't been used to drinking much normally, and all she could remember was standing up at one point and feeling very dizzy. One of her colleagues had taken her outside to get some air. And it was then that he had tried to kiss her.

At first Julia had rejected his advances, but he'd been persistent…and that awful insecurity had risen up. What if Kaden had finished with her without even telling her? What if he wasn't even going to say goodbye to her? Even stronger had been the rising sense of desperation to think that Kaden might be the only man who would ever make her feel whole, who would ever be able to awaken her sensuality. The thought of being beholden to one man who didn't want her terrified her. The way she'd come to depend on Kaden, to love him, had raised all her very private fears and vulnerabilities about being adopted…and rejection.

He *couldn't* be the only one who would ever make

her feel anything again, she'd determined. So she had allowed that man to kiss her—almost in an attempt to prove something to herself.

It had been an effort in futility from the first moment, making instant nausea rise.

And that was when she'd seen Kaden, across the dark street, in long robes and looking half wild, with stubble darkening his jaw. She'd been so shocked she hadn't been able to move, and then…too late…she'd started to struggle. Kaden had just looked at her with those dark implacable eyes, and then he'd turned and left.

The following day the death of Kaden's father had been announced.

Only by refusing to move from outside the state offices had Julia eventually been allowed to see Kaden before she left the country a few days later. She'd stepped into a huge, opulent office to see Kaden standing in the middle of the room, legs splayed, dressed in ceremonial robes, gorgeous and formidable. And like an utter stranger.

She'd been incredibly nervous. "Kaden… I…" She'd never found it hard to speak with him, not from the moment they'd first met, but suddenly she struggled to get two words out. "I'm so sorry about your father."

"Thank you." His voice was clipped. Curt.

"I…I've tried to see you before now, but you've been busy."

His mouth thinned. "From the looks of things you've been busy yourself."

Julia flushed brick red when she remembered her tangled emotions and what they'd led her to do. "What you saw the other night…it was nothing. I'd had a bit too much to drink and—"

Kaden lifted a hand, an expression of distaste etched on his face. "Please, spare me the sordid details. It does not interest me in the slightest how or when or where you made love to that man."

Julia protested. "We didn't make love. It was just a stupid kiss… It stopped almost as soon as it had started."

Kaden's voice was icy. "Like I said, I'm really not interested. Now, what was it you wanted to see me about? As you said yourself, I'm very busy."

Julia immediately felt ashamed. Kaden was grieving.

"I just…I wanted to give you my condolences personally and to say…goodbye. I'm leaving tomorrow."

A layer of shock was making her a little numb. Not so long ago this man had held her in his arms underneath a blanket of stars and said to her fervently, "*I love you. I won't ever love another woman again.*"

Nausea surged, and Julia had to put her hands against the shower wall and breathe deep. She hadn't thought of that awful evening for a long time.

And yet it wouldn't go away, the memory as stubborn as a dark stain. She could remember feeling compelled to blurt out, "Kaden…why are you behaving like this?"

He'd arched a brow and crossed his arms. "Like what?"

"Like you hardly know me."

His face had been a mask of cool civility. "You think six months of a summer fling means that I *know* you?"

Julia could remember flinching so violently that she'd taken a step backwards. "I didn't think of it as a fling. I thought what we had was—"

He had slashed down a hand, stopping her words, his face suddenly fierce. "What we had was an affair, Julia. Nothing more and nothing less than what you were engaging in with that man the other night. You are not from this world." His mouth had curled up in an awful parody of a mocking smile, "You didn't seriously think that you would ever become a permanent part of it, did you?"

Of course she hadn't. But her conscience niggled her. Deep within her, in a very secret place, she'd harboured a dream that perhaps this was *it*. He'd even mentioned his London apartment. Bile rose as she acknowledged that perhaps all he'd meant by that was that he'd give her the role of convenient mistress.

Horror spread through her body as the awful reality sank in. It was written all over every rejecting and rigid line of his body. Everything she'd shared with Kaden had been a mere illusion. He'd been playing with her. A western student girl, here for a short while and then conveniently gone. Perfect for a summer fling. And now he was ruler, a million miles from the carefree young man she thought she'd known.

Shakily she said, "You didn't have to tell me you loved me. You could have spared yourself the platitudes. I didn't expect to hear them." And she hadn't. She truly hadn't. She knew she loved this man, but she hadn't expected him to love her back…and yet he had. Or so she'd been led to believe.

Kaden shrugged and looked at a cuff, as if it was infinitely more interesting than their conversation. He looked back at her with eyes so black they were dead. "I went as far as you did. Please don't insult my intelligence and tell me that you meant it when *you* said it. You can hardly claim you did when within days you were ready to drop your pants for another man."

Julia backed away again at his crude words, shaking

her head this time, eyes horrifically glued to Kaden. "I told you, it wasn't like that."

She realised in that moment that she'd not ever known this man. And with that came the insidious feeling of worthlessness she'd carried ever since she'd found out she was adopted and that her own birth mother had rejected her. She wasn't good enough for anyone. She never had been…

To this day Julia couldn't actually remember walking out of that room, or the night that had followed, or the journey to the airport the next day. She only remembered being back in grey, drizzly autumnal England and feeling as though her insides had been ripped out and trampled on. The feeling of rejection was like a corrosive acid, eating away at her, and for a long time she hadn't trusted her own judgement when it came to men. She'd locked herself away in her studies.

Her husband John had managed to break through her wall of defences with his gentle, unassuming ways, but Julia could see now that she'd fallen for him precisely because he'd been everything Kaden was *not*.

When she thought of what had happened last night, and Kaden's cool assertion that he would see her later—exactly the way a man might talk to a mistress—nausea surged again, and this time Julia couldn't hold it down. She made it to the toilet in time and was violently ill. When she was able to, she stood and looked at herself in the mirror. She was deathly pale, eyes huge.

What cruel twist of fate had brought them together like this again?

And yet even now, with the memory of how brutally he'd rejected her still acrid like the bile in her throat, Julia felt a helpless weakness invade her. And, worse, that insidious yearning. Shakily she sat down on the closed toilet seat and vowed to herself that she would thwart Kaden's arrogant assumption that she would fall in with his plans. Because she didn't know if she could survive standing in front of him again when he was finished with her, and hearing him tell her it was over.

CHAPTER FIVE

KADEN sat in his car outside Julia's modest-sized townhouse. He was oblivious to the fact that his stately vehicle looked ridiculously out of place in the leafy residential street. His mind and belly were churning and had been all day. Much to his intense chagrin he hadn't been able to concentrate on the business at hand at all, causing his staff to look worried. He was *never* distracted.

He'd struggled to find some sense of equilibrium. But equilibrium had taken a hike and in its place was an ever-present gnawing knowledge that he'd been here before. In this place, standing at the edge of an abyss. About to disappear.

Kaden's hand tightened to a fist on his thigh. He was not that young man any more. He'd lived and married and divorced. He'd had lovers—many lovers. And not one woman had come close to touching that part of him that he'd locked away years before. When Julia had turned and walked out of his study.

He shook his head to dislodge the memory, but it wouldn't budge. That last meeting was engraved in his mind like a tattoo. Julia's slate-grey eyes wide, her cheeks pale as she'd listened to what he'd said. The burning jealousy in his gut when he'd thought of her with that man. It had eclipsed even his grief at his father's death. The realisation that she was fallible, that she was like every other woman, had been the start of his cynicism.

Most mocking of all though—even now—was the memory of why he'd gone looking for her on that cataclysmic night of his father's death. Contrary to his father's repeated wishes, Kaden had insisted that he wanted Julia. He'd gone to find her, to explain his absence and also to tell her that he wanted her to be his queen some day. That he was prepared to let her finish her studies and get used to the idea and then make a choice. Fired up with love—*or so he'd thought*—he hadn't been prepared for seeing her entangled in that embrace, outside in the street, where anyone could have seen her. *His woman.*

He could remember feeling disembodied. He could remember the way something inside him had shrivelled up to nothing as he'd watched her finally notice him and start to struggle. In that moment whatever he'd felt for her had solidified to a hard black mass within him, and then it had been buried for good.

Only a scant hour later, when Kaden had sat by his dying father's bed and he had begged Kaden to "*think of your country, not yourself*", Kaden had finally seen the future clearly. And that future did not include Julia.

It had been a summer of madness. Of believing feelings existed just because they'd been each other's first lover. He'd come close to believing he loved her, but had realised just in time that he'd confused lust and sexual obsession with love.

As if waking from a dream, Kaden came back to the car, to the street in suburban London. He looked at the townhouse. Benign and peaceful. His blood thickened and grew hot. Inside that house was the woman who stood between him and his future. On some level he'd never really let her go, and the only way he could do that was to sate this beast inside him. Prove that it was lust once and for all. And this time when he said goodbye to her she would no longer have the power to make him wake, sweating, from vivid dreams, holding a hand to his chest to assuage the dull ache.

Julia felt as if she was thirteen all over again, with butterflies in her belly, flushing hot and cold every two seconds. She'd heard Kaden's car pull up and her nerves were wound taut waiting for the doorbell. What was he doing? she wondered for the umpteenth time, when he still didn't emerge from the huge car.

Then she imagined it pulling away again, and didn't like the feeling of panic *that* engendered. She'd vacillated all day over what to do, all the while knowing, to her ongoing sense of shame, that she'd somewhere along the way made up her mind that she wasn't strong enough to walk away from Kaden.

By the time she'd returned from work, with a splitting headache, she'd felt cranky enough with herself for being so weak that she'd decided she *wouldn't* give in so easily. She would greet Kaden in her running sweats and tell him she wasn't going anywhere. But then she'd had an image of him clicking his fingers, having food delivered to the house and staying all night. She couldn't forget the glint of determination in his eye that morning. And the thought of having him here in her private space for a whole night had been enough to galvanise her into getting dressed in a plain black dress and smart pumps.

The lesser of two evils was to let him take her out.

She'd thank him for dinner, tell him that there couldn't possibly be a repeat of last night, and that would be it. She'd never see him again. She was strong enough to do this.

She'd turned away from her furtive vigil at the window for a moment, so she nearly jumped out of her skin when the doorbell rang authoritatively. And all her previous thoughts were scrambled into a million pieces. Her hands were clammy. Her heart thumped. She walked to the front door and could see the looming tall, dark shape through the bubbled glass. She picked up her bag and cardigan and took a deep breath.

When she opened the door she wasn't prepared for the hit to her gut at seeing a stubble-jawed Kaden leaning nonchalantly against the porch wall, dominating the small space. He obviously hadn't shaved since that morning, and flames of heat licked through her blood. He was so intensely masculine. He was in the same suit—albeit with the tie gone and the top button of his shirt open.

His eyes were dark and swept her up and down as he straightened up. She tingled all over. Julia wished she'd put her hair up, it felt provocative now to have it down. Why had she left it down?

Kaden arched a brow. "Shall we?"

Julia sucked in a breath and finally managed to move. "Yes…" She pulled the front door behind her, absurdly glad that Kaden hadn't come inside, and fumbled with the keys as she locked it. Kaden was waiting by the door of the car and helped her in. His hand was hot on her bare elbow.

The car pulled off smoothly and Julia tried to quell her butterflies. Kaden's drawling and unmistakably amused voice came from her right.

"Are we going to a funeral?"

She looked at him and could see him staring pointedly at her admittedly rather boring dress. She fibbed. "I didn't have time to change after work."

His eyes rose to hers and he smiled. "Liar," he mocked softly.

Julia was transfixed by that smiling mouth, by the unbelievably sensuous and wicked lines. Her face flamed and her hand moved in that betraying reflex to her throat. She stopped herself just in time. She felt naked without his necklace. It was the first time she'd not worn it at home. Her hand dropped to her lap, and to hide her discomfiture she asked, "Where are we going?"

To her relief Kaden released her from his all too intent gaze and looked ahead. "We're going to the Cedar Rooms, in the Gormseby Hotel."

Julia was impressed. It was a plush new hotel that had opened in the past few months, and apparently there was already a year-long waiting list for the restaurant. Not for Kaden, though, she thought cynically. They'd be tripping over themselves to have him endorse their restaurant. Yet she was relieved at the idea of being in a public place, surrounded by people, as if that would somehow help her resist him and put up the fight she knew she must.

Kaden was struggling to hang on to his urbanity beside Julia. Her dress was ridiculously boring and plain, but it couldn't hide her effortless class, or those long shapely legs and the enticing swell of her bosom. Her hair was down, falling in long waves over her shoulders, and she wore a minimum of make-up. Once again he was struck that she could pass for years younger. And y how beautiful she was. She had the kind of classic beauty that just got better with age.

The minute she'd opened the front door her huge swirling grey eyes had sucked him into a vortex of need so strong that he'd felt his body responding right there. Much as it had in that crowded room last night. A response he'd never had to curb for any other woman, because he'd always been in strict control.

With Julia, though, his brain short-circuited every time he looked at her. It only fired up his assertion that this was just lust. With that in mind, and anticipating how urgent his desire would be by the time they got to dessert, he made a quick terse call in Arabic from his mobile phone.

By the time they were on their desserts Julia had given up trying to maintain any kind of coherent conversation. The opulent dining room was arranged in such a way that—far from being surrounded by the public—she and Kaden were practically in a private booth. And it was so dark that flickering candles sent long shadows across their faces. It was decadent, and not at all conducive to remaining clear-headed as she'd anticipated.

Their conversation had started out innocuously enough. Kaden had asked her about her career and why she'd taken the direction she had. She'd explained that her passion for fund distribution had grown when she'd seen so much misused funding over the years, and she'd seen it as the more stable end of archaeology, considering her future with a husband and family. To her surprise his eyes hadn't glazed over with boredom. He'd kept looking at her, though, as if he wanted to devour her. Desperately trying to ignore the way it made her feel, she'd asked him about Burquat.

It sounded like another country now—vastly different from the more rigidly conservative one she'd known. Once again she was filled with a rush of pride that his ambition was being realised.

Scrabbling around for anything else to talk about, to take the edge off how intimate it felt to be sitting here with him, Julia said, "I saw something in the papers about drilling your oil-fields. There seems to be great interest, considering the world's dwindling oil supplies."

"We're certainly on the brink of something huge. Sultan Sadiq of Al-Omar is going to help us drill the oil. He has the expertise."

"Is that part of the reason why he's marrying Samia?" Julia felt a pang of concern for Kaden's younger sister. From what she remembered of her she was no match for the renowned playboy Sultan.

Kaden's mouth tightened. "It's a factor, yes. Their marriage will be an important strategic alliance between both our countries."

Kaden sat back and cradled a bulbous glass of brandy. He looked at Julia from under hooded lids. She felt hunted.

"So…your boss—Nigel. Are you seeing him?"

Julia flushed, wondering what kind of woman Kaden had become used to socialising with, *sleeping* with. She swallowed. "No, I'm not." Not sure why she felt compelled to elaborate, she said, "He's asked me out, but I've said no."

"You've had no lovers since your husband?"

Julia flushed even hotter and glared at Kaden. "That's

none of your business. Would you mind if I asked *you* if you've had any lovers since your divorce?"

He was supremely relaxed, supremely confident. He smiled. "I have a healthy sex life. I enjoy women…and they enjoy what I can give them."

Julia snorted indelicately, her imagination shamefully providing her with an assortment of images of the sleek, soignée women she'd seen grace his arm over the years. "No doubt." And then something dark was rising up within her, and she said ascerbically, "I presume these women are left in no doubt as to the parameters of their relationship with you, much as you outlined to me this morning?"

Kaden's face darkened ominously. "I took your advice a long time ago. Women know exactly where they stand with me. I don't waste my breath on platitudes and empty promises."

For some perverse reason Julia felt inexplicably comforted. As if Kaden had just proved to her that no woman had managed to break through that wall of ice. And yet…how would *she* know? She was the last woman in the world he would confide in. And she was obviously the last woman in the world who could break through the icy reserve she'd seen that last evening in Burquat.

She realised then just how provocative the conversation was becoming, and put down her napkin. "I think I'm ready to go now."

Kaden rose smoothly to his feet and indicated for Julia to precede him out of the booth. With his head inclined solicitously he was urbanity incarnate, but Julia didn't trust it for a second. She knew the dark, seething passion that hummed between them was far from over.

When they reached the lobby Julia turned towards

the main door, her mind was whirring with ways to say goodbye to Kaden and insist on getting a taxi. At the same time her belly was clenching pathetically at the thought of never seeing him again. Kaden caught her hand and her mind blanked at the physical contact. She looked up at him, and that slow lick of desire coiled through her belly. She cursed it—and herself.

"I've booked a suite here for the night."

Julia straightened her spine and tried to block out the tantalising suggestion that they could be in bed within minutes. "If your aim is to make me feel like a high-class hooker then you're succeeding admirably."

Kaden cursed himself. Never before had he lacked finesse with a woman. He wanted Julia so badly he ached, and he'd booked the room because he'd known he wouldn't have the restraint to wait until he got back to his apartment or her house. But she was as stiff as a board and about as remote as the summit of Everest. He had a good idea that she had every intention of walking away from him. He didn't like the dart of panic he felt at acknowledging that.

Julia watched Kaden's face. It was expressionless except for his jaw clenching and his eyes flashing. A dart of panic rose; to willingly spend another night with this man was emotional suicide.

"Kaden, I don't know what you think you're doing, but I came here tonight to have dinner with you. I do not intend repeating what happened last night. There's no point. We have nothing to say to each other."

In a move so fast her head spun, he was right in front of her. He said roughly, "*We* may have nothing to say to each other, but our bodies have plenty to say."

He put his hands on her arms and pulled her close.

She sucked in a breath when she felt the burgeoning response of his body against her. Immediately there was an exultant rush of blood to her groin in answer. Any thoughts of emotional suicide were fading fast.

And it was then that she noticed they were standing in the middle of the lobby and attracting attention. How could they not? Kaden was six feet four at least, and one of the most recognisable men on the planet. Even if he wasn't, his sheer good looks would draw enough attention.

He intuited the direction of her thoughts, and his eyes glinted down at her. "I have no problem making love to you here and now, Julia."

To illustrate his point he pulled her in even tighter and brought his mouth down so close that she could feel his breath feather along her lips. Instinctively her mouth was already opening, seeking his.

He whispered, "We have unfinished business, Julia. Are you really ready to walk away from this? Because I'm not."

And with that he settled his mouth over hers, right in the middle of that exclusive lobby, in front of all those moneyed people. But for all Julia was aware they might have been in her house. What undid her completely was that his kiss was gentle and restrained, but she could feel the barely leashed passion behind it. If he'd been forceful it would have been easier to resist, but this kiss reminded her too much of the Kaden she'd once known…

His hands moved up to cradle her face, holding her in place while his tongue delved deep and stroked along hers, making her gasp with need.

Eventually he drew back and said, "The reason I booked the room was because I knew I wouldn't be able to wait until I got you home. Not because I wanted you to feel like a high-class call girl. Now, we can continue this where we stand, and give the guests the show of their lives, or we can go upstairs."

Julia's hands had crept up to cling onto Kaden's arms. She felt the muscles bunch and move and looked up into those dark eyes. She could feel herself falling down and down. There was no space between them. No space to think. She didn't have the strength to walk away. Not yet.

Hating herself, she said shakily, "OK. Upstairs."

With grim determination stamped all over his darkly gorgeous features, Kaden held her close and walked her across the lobby to the lifts. Her face flamed when she became aware of people's discreet scrutiny, and Julia realised that within the space of twenty-four hours her carefully ordered and structured life had come tumbling down around her ears—so much so that she didn't even recognise herself any more.

And the worst thing about this whole scenario: she was exhilarated in a way she hadn't felt in a long time.

For the second morning in a row Julia woke up in an unfamiliar room and bed. But this time there was no pristine Kaden in a suit, watching her as she woke. The bed beside her was empty, sheets well tousled. She knew instantly that she was alone, and didn't like the bereft feeling that took her by surprise. Their scent mingled with the air, along with the scent of sex. In a flash the previous night came back in glorious Technicolor.

They'd said not a word once they'd got to the room. They'd been naked and in bed within seconds, mutually combusting.

They'd made love for hours, insatiably. Hungering for one another only moments after each completion. Julia was exhausted, but she couldn't deny the illicit feeling of peace within her. She sighed deeply. She knew Kaden was going to Al-Omar the next day for Samia's wedding.

Then she spotted something out of the corner of her eye. She turned her head to see a folded piece of stiff hotel paper. She opened it up and read the arrogantly slashing handwriting: *I'll pick you up at your place, 7.30. K*

Julia sighed again. One more night in this strange week when everything felt out of kilter and off balance and slightly dream-like. She'd love to be able to send a terse note back with a curt dismissal, but if last night had proved anything it was that the fire had well and truly been stoked and she was too fatally weak to resist. All of the very good reasons she had for saying no—her very self-preservation, for a start—were awfully elusive at the prospect of seeing Kaden for a last time.

When the doorbell rang that evening Julia was flustered. She opened the door, and once again wasn't prepared for the effect of the reality of Kaden on her doorstep.

"Hi… Look, I've just got back from work." She indicated her uniform of trousers, shirt and flat shoes. "I need to shower and change. Today was busy, and then there was a problem with the tube line, and—" She stopped abruptly. She was babbling. As if he cared about the vagaries of public transport.

Kaden took a step inside her door before she knew what was happening, dwarfing her small hallway, and said easily, "We're in no rush. You get ready; I'll wait down here."

Julia gulped, and her hand went nervously to her

throat again. But of course the necklace wasn't there. Every morning she had to consciously remember not to put it on. Self-recrimination at her own weakness made her say curtly, "I won't be long. There's fresh coffee in the kitchen if you want to help yourself."

And with that she fled upstairs and locked herself into her *en suite* bedroom. Lord, she was in trouble.

Kaden prowled through the hallway. From what he could see it was a classic two-up-two-down house, with a bright airy kitchen extending at the back, which was obviously a modern addition. He hated this weakness he felt for the woman upstairs. Even now he wanted to follow her into the shower and embed himself in her tight heat.

Last night had been very far removed from the nights he'd shared with other women. He was always quickly sated and eager to see them leave, or leave himself. But it had only been as dawn was breaking and his body was too weak to continue that he'd finally fallen asleep.

When he'd woken a couple of hours later all he'd had to do was look at Julia's sleeping body to want to wake her and start all over again. Right now he didn't feel as if an entire month locked in a hotel room would be enough to rid him of this need.

His mind shied away from that realisation, and from more introspection. It was perhaps inevitable that his first lover should make a lasting impression, leave a mark on his soul. The chemistry between them had been intense from the moment they'd met over that fossil at the city dig. Kaden's mouth twisted. It had been as if he'd been infected with a fever, becoming so obsessed with Julia and having her that he hadn't been able to see anything else.

He hadn't even noticed his own father's growing frailty. Nor even listened to his father's pleas until they'd been uttered with his last breath.

With a curse he turned away from the view of the tiny but perfect garden. What was he doing here, in this small suburban house? His movements jerky, he found a cup and poured himself a strong black coffee, as if that might untangle the knots in his head and belly.

He wandered through to the bright and minimalist sitting-room. He wondered, with an acidic taste in his mouth, if this had been the marital home. He couldn't see any wedding photos anywhere, but stopped dead when he saw the panoramic photo hanging above the fireplace, his insides freezing in shock.

It was a familiar view—one of his favourites. A picture taken in the Burquati desert, with the stunning snow-capped Nazish mountain range in the distance. He had a vivid memory of the day Julia had taken this picture. His arms had been tight around her waist and she'd complained throatily, "I can't keep the camera steady if you hang onto me like you're drowning!"

And he'd said into her ear, overcome with emotion, "I'm drowning, all right. In love with you."

The shutter had clicked at that moment, and then she'd turned in his arms and—

"I'm sorry—I tried to be as quick as I could."

Kaden's hand gripped the coffee mug so tightly he had to consciously relax for fear of breaking it into pieces. He schooled his features so they were a bland mask which reflected nothing of his inner reaction to the memory sparked by the picture.

He turned around. Julia was wearing a dark grey silky dress that dipped down at the front to reveal her delicate collarbone and clung to the soft swells of her breasts, dropping in soft, unstructured folds to her knee. Her legs were bare and pale, and she wore high-heeled wedges. He dragged his eyes up to hers. She'd tied her hair back into a ponytail and it made her look ridiculously innocent and young.

Julia's body was reacting with irritating predictability to Kaden's searing look. When she'd walked in she'd noted with dismay that he'd spotted the photograph. It was one of her favourite possessions. Her husband John had used to complain about it, having taken an instant dislike to it, and she'd hidden it away during their marriage. It was almost as if he'd intuited that she'd lost her heart in that very desert. At that very moment.

Kaden indicated behind him now, without taking his dark eyes off hers. "The frame suits the photo. It turned out well."

She fixed a bright smile on her face, resolutely blocking out the memory of that day. "Yes, it did. I'm ready to go."

Kaden looked at her for a long moment and then threw back the rest of his coffee. He went into the kitchen, where he put the cup in the sink, rinsed it, and then came into the hall. Julia already had the door open, and allowed Kaden to precede her out so she could lock up.

Like the previous night, she asked him, once in the back of the car, "Where are we going?"

"I thought we'd go to my apartment this evening. I've arranged for a Burquati chef to cook dinner. I thought you might appreciate being reminded of some of our local dishes."

Sounding a little strangled, Julia answered, "That sounds nice."

* * *

And it was. Julia savoured every morsel of the delicious food. She'd always loved it. Balls of rice mixed with succulent pieces of lamb and fish. Tender chicken breasts marinaded for hours in spices. Fresh vegetables fried in tantalising Burquati oils. And decadent sweet pastries dripping with syrup for dessert, washed down with tart black coffee.

"You haven't lost your appetite."

Julia looked across the small intimate table at Kaden. He was lounging back in his chair like a sleek panther, in a dark shirt and black trousers. She felt hot, and her hand went in that telling gesture to her neck again. She dropped it quickly. "No. I've never lost my healthy appetite." She smiled ruefully and the action felt strange. She realized she hadn't smiled much in the past few days. "That's why I run six miles about three times a week—to be able to indulge the foodie within me."

Kaden's eyes roved over her. "You were definitely a little…plumper before."

There was a rough quality to his voice that resonated deep inside Julia. She could remember Kaden's hands squeezing her breasts together, lavishing attention on the voluptuous mounds.

"Puppy fat," she said, almost desperately.

Abruptly she stood up, agitated, and took her glass of wine to go and stand by the open doors of the dining room, which led out to an ornate terraced balcony overlooking the city. She needed air and space. He was too intense and brooding. The tension between them, all that was not being acknowledged about their past history, was nearly suffocating. And yet what was there to say? Julia certainly didn't need to hear Kaden elaborate again on why he'd been so keen to see the back of her…

She heard him move and come to stand beside her. She took a careful sip of wine, trying to be as nonchalant as possible, but already she was trembling with wanting him just to take her in his arms and make her forget everything. One last night and then she would put him out of her mind for good.

"I want you to come to Al-Omar with me for Samia's wedding."

Julia's head whipped round so fast she felt dizzy for a moment. "What?" she squeaked, "You want me to come…as your date?"

He was looking impossibly grim, which made Julia believe that she hadn't just had an aural hallucination. He nodded. "It'll be over by Sunday."

Julia felt bewildered. She hadn't prepared emotionally for anything beyond this night. "But…why?"

Kaden's jaw tightened. He wasn't sure, but he was damn hopeful it would mean the end of his burning need to take this woman every time he looked at her. And that it would make all the old memories recede to a place where they would have no hold over him any more. That it would bring him to a place where he could get on with his life and not be haunted by her and the nebulous feeling of something having gone very wrong twelve years before.

He shrugged. "I thought you might enjoy meeting Samia again."

Julia looked at Kaden warily. His expression gave nothing away, but there was a starkness to the lines of his face, a hunger. She recognised it because she felt it too. The thought of *this*—whatever it was between them—lasting for another few days out of time was all at once heady and terrifying.

She'd once longed for him to come after her, to tell her he'd made a mistake. That he *did* love her. But he hadn't. Now he wanted to spend more time with her. Perhaps this was as close as she would ever get to closure? This man had haunted her for too long.

She stared down at her wine glass as if the ruby liquid held all the answers. "I don't know, Kaden…" She looked back up. "I don't know if it's such a good idea."

Kaden sneaked a hand out and around the back of her neck. Gently he urged her closer to him, as if he could tell that her words were a pathetic attempt to pretend she didn't want this.

"This is desire—karma—unfinished business. Call it what you will, but whatever it is it's powerful. And it's not over."

Kaden's hand was massaging the back of her neck now, and Julia felt like purring and turning her face into his palm. She gritted her jaw. "I have to work tomorrow. I can't just up and leave the country. I'll…have to think about it."

His eyes flashed. Clearly he was unused to anything less than immediate acquiescence. "You can do whatever you want, Julia. You're beholden to none. But while you're thinking about it, think about *this*."

This was Kaden removing the wine glass from her hand and pulling her into him so tightly that she could feel every hard ridge of muscle and the powerful thrust of his thighs and manhood. Cradling her face in his hands, he swooped—and obliterated every thought in her head with his kiss.

CHAPTER SIX

"WOULD you like some champagne, Dr Somerton?"

Julia looked at the impeccably made-up Burquati air hostess and decided she could so with a little fortitude. She smiled tightly. "Yes, please."

The woman expertly filled a real crystal flute with champagne, and then passed a glass of what looked like brandy to Kaden, who sat across the aisle of his own private jet.

It was dark outside. It would take roughly six hours to get to B'harani, the capital of Al-Omar. They'd been scheduled to leave that afternoon, but Kaden had been held up with business matters—hence their overnight flight.

Julia's brain was already slipping helplessly back into the well-worn groove that it had trod all day. *Why* had she decided to come? A flush went through her body when she remembered back to that morning, as dawn had been breaking. She'd been exhausted. Kaden had been ruthless and remorseless all night. Each orgasm had felt like another brick dismantled in the wall of her defences.

Kaden had hovered over her and asked throatily, "So, will you come to Al-Omar with me?"

Julia had sensed in him a tiny moment of such fleeting vulnerability that she must have imagined it, but it had got to her, stripping away any remaining defences. Stripping away her automatic response to say no and do the right thing, the logical thing. Lying there naked, she'd been at his mercy. To her ongoing shame, she'd just nodded her head weakly, reminding herself that this was finite and soon she would be back to normal, hopefully a little freer of painful memories.

"You don't need to look like you're about to walk the plank. You're going to be a guest at the society wedding of the year."

Julia clutched the glass tightly in her hand now and looked at Kaden. Since she'd got into his car just a couple of hours ago outside her house he'd been on the phone. And he'd been engrossed in his laptop since boarding the flight. But now he was looking at her.

Unbidden, the words tumbled out. "Why are you doing this? Why are we here?" *Why have you come back into my life to tear me open all over again? And, worse, why am I allowing it to happen?*

It was as if she had to hear him reiterate the reasons why she was being so stupid. Kaden's dark eyes held hers for a long moment and then dropped in a leisurely appraisal of her body. Julia was modestly dressed: a plain shirt tucked into high-waisted flared trousers. Her hair was coiled back into a chignon. It should have felt like armour, but it didn't. Kaden's laser-like gaze had the power to make her feel naked.

His eyes met hers again. "We are doing this to sate the desire between us. We're two consenting adults taking pleasure in one another. Nothing more, nothing less."

Julia swallowed painfully. "There's more to it than

that, Kaden. We have a past together. Something you seem determined to ignore."

Kaden turned more fully in his seat, and Julia felt threatened when she saw how cynicism stamped the lines of his face. And something else—something much darker. Anger.

"I fail to see what talking about the past will serve. We had an affair aeons ago. We're different people now. The only constant is that we still want each other."

Affair. Julia cursed herself for opening her mouth. Kaden was right. What on earth could they possibly have to talk about? She was humiliatingly aware that she wanted him to tell her that he hadn't meant to reject her so brutally. She didn't feel like a different person. She felt as if she was twenty all over again and nothing had changed.

Incredibly brittle, and angry for having exposed herself like this, she forced a smile. "You're right. I'm tired. It's been a long day."

Kaden frowned now, and his eyes went to her throat. "Why do you keep doing that? Touching your neck as if you're looking for something?"

Julia gulped, and realised that once again in an unconsciously nervous gesture her hand had sought out the comforting touch of her necklace. Panic flared. She wasn't wearing it, but she'd broken her own rule and brought it with her, like some kind of talisman. She blushed. "It's just a habit…a necklace I used to wear. I lost it some time ago and I haven't got used to it being gone yet."

His eyes narrowed on her and, feeling panicky, Julia put down her glass and started to recline her chair. "I think I'll try to get some sleep."

Kaden felt the bitter sting of a memory, and with it an emotion he refused to acknowledge. It was too piercing. He'd once given Julia a necklace, but he had no doubt that wasn't the necklace she referred to. It was probably some delicate diamond thing her husband had bought her.

The one he'd given her would be long gone. What woman would hold on to a cheap gold necklace bought in a marketplace on a whim because he'd felt that the knot in the design symbolised the intricacies of his emotions for his lover? His lover. Julia. Then and now.

He cursed himself and turned away to look out at the inky blackness. He should have walked away from her in London this morning and come to Al-Omar to make a fresh start. He needed to look for a new bride to take him into the next phase of his life. He needed to create the family legacy he'd promised his father, and an economically and politically stable country. It was all within his grasp finally, after long years of work and struggle and one disastrous marriage.

He glanced back to Julia's curved waist and hips and his blood grew hot. He still wanted her, though. She was unfinished business. His hands clenched. He couldn't take one step into the future while this hunger raged within him and it *would* be sated. It had to be.

Arriving in B'harani as dawn broke was breathtaking. The gleaming city was bathed in a pinky pearlescent light. It was festooned with flags and decorations, and streets were cordoned off for the first wedding procession, which would take place later that day.

Kaden had barely shared one word with Julia as they'd sped through the streets to the imposing Hussein Castle.

There, they'd been shown to their opulent suite, and Kaden had excused himself to go and see his sister.

Now Julia was alone in the room, gritty-eyed with tiredness and a little numb at acknowledging that she was back on the Arabian Peninsula with Kaden. She succumbed to the lure of a shower and afterwards put on a luxurious towelling robe. The massive bed dressed in white Egyptian cotton was beckoning, and she lay down with the intention of having a quick nap.

When she woke, some time later, the sun was high outside and she felt very disoriented when she saw Kaden emerge from the bathroom with a tiny towel slung around his hips. He was rubbing his hair with another towel, and he was a picture of dark olive-skinned virility, muscles bunching and gleaming.

Julia sat up awkwardly. "Why didn't you wake me?"

He cast her a quick glance. "You were exhausted. There's nothing much happening till this evening anyway. The civil ceremony took place this morning, and Sultan Sadiq and Samia are doing a procession through the streets this afternoon. This evening will be the formal start of the celebrations, with more over the next two days. On Sunday they will marry again in a more western style."

"Wow," breathed Julia, while trying to ignore the sight of Kaden's half naked body, "That sounds complicated."

Kaden smiled tightly, seemingly unaware of his state of undress. He flung aside the towel he'd been drying his hair with, leaving it sexily dishevelled. "Yes, quite. In Burquat things are much more straightforward. We just have a wedding ceremony in front of our elders at dawn and then a huge ceremonial banquet which lasts all day."

Against her best effort to focus on what he was saying, Julia couldn't stop her gaze from dropping down Kaden's exquisitely muscled chest. He really had the most amazing body—huge but leanly muscled. The towel around his hips looked very precarious, and as she watched, wide-eyed, she could see the distinctive bulge grow visibly bigger.

Her cheeks flamed and her gaze jumped up to meet Kaden's much more mocking one. His hand whipped aside the towel and it fell to the floor along with the other one. Gulping, she watched as he walked to the bed. He lay alongside her and pushed aside the robe, baring her breasts to his gaze. Once again Julia was a little stunned at this much more sexually confident Kaden and how intoxicating he was.

Weakly, she tried to protest, "What if someone comes in?"

"They won't," he growled, and bent his head to surround one tight nipple with hot, wet, sucking heat.

Julia moaned and collapsed back completely. Kaden's other hand slid down her belly, undoing the tie on the robe as he dipped lower and between her legs, to where she was already indecently wet and ready.

He removed the robe and within seconds she was naked too, with Kaden's body settled between her legs, his shoulders huge above her. She could feel him flex the taut muscles of his behind and widened her legs, inviting him into more intimate contact. When he thrust into her Julia had to close her eyes, because she was terrified he would see the emotion boiling in her chest. As he started up with a delicious rhythm Julia desperately assured herself that this was just about sex, not emotion. She didn't love him any more. She couldn't… Because if she did, the emotional carnage was too scary to contemplate.

Later that evening Julia paced the sitting room, barely aware of the gorgeous cream and gold furnishings, carpet so thick her heels sank into it.

She'd been whisked off that afternoon to be pampered in readiness for the banquet—something she hadn't expected. And while there she'd had a selection of outfits for her to pick from. Too unsure to know whether or not she could refuse, she'd chosen the simplest gown. Deep green in colour, it was halter-necked, with a daringly low-cut back. She'd been returned to the suite and now, made-up and with her hair in an elaborate chignon, she felt like a veritable fashion doll.

And there was no sign of Kaden. Julia paced some more. Being dressed up like this made her intensely uncomfortable. She'd caught a glimpse of herself in the mirror and for a moment hadn't even recognised the image reflected back. Her eyes were huge and smoky grey, lashes long and very black. Her cheeks had two spots of red that had more to do with her emotions than with artifice.

The door suddenly clicked, and Julia whirled around to see Kaden striding in, adjusting a cufflink on his shirt. The breath literally left her throat for a moment. It was the first time she'd ever seen him in a tuxedo and he looked…stunning. It nearly made her forget why she was so incensed, but then he looked at her with that irritating non-expression. The irrational feeling of anger surged back.

She gestured to the dress. "I agreed to come with you to a wedding. I'm not your mistress, Kaden, and I don't appreciate being treated like one."

He put his hands in his pockets and looked her up and down, and then, as if he hadn't even heard her, he said, "I've never seen you look so beautiful."

To Julia's abject horror her mind emptied and she stood there, stupidly, as Kaden's black gaze fused with hers. She read the heat in its glowing depths. She'd always veered more towards being a tomboy, and had truly never felt especially *beautiful*. But now, here in this room, she did.

It made the bright spark of anger fade away, and she felt silly for her outburst. Of course Kaden didn't see her as his mistress. She couldn't be further removed from the kind of women he sought out.

She half gestured to the dress, avoiding Kaden's eye. "I didn't mean to sound ungrateful. It's a lovely dress, and the attention…wasn't all bad." She looked back up. "But I don't want you to get the wrong idea. I don't expect or even want this kind of treatment. I'm not like your other women. This…what's happening here…is not the same…"

He took his hands out of his pockets and came close. Julia stood her ground, but it was hard. Black eyes glittered down into hers. A muscle throbbed in his jaw and she saw how tightly Kaden was reining in some explosive emotion.

"No, you're not like my other women. You're completely different. Don't think I'm not aware of that. Now, let's go or we'll be late."

After a tense moment she finally moved. Kaden stood back and allowed Julia to precede him out of the room.

Feeling off-centre, he didn't touch her as they walked down the long corridor. She wasn't and hadn't ever been like any other woman he'd been with. It was only now that he was noticing the disturbing tendency he'd always had to judge the women he encountered against his first lover—noticing the faint disappointment he always felt when they proved themselves time and time again to be utterly different. Materialistic. Avaricious. *Less.*

He was used to being ecstatically received whenever he indulged a woman, and wondered if this was some ploy or game Julia was playing—affecting uninterest. But with a sinking feeling he knew it wasn't. Years ago she'd have laughed in his face if he'd so much as attempted to get her into a couture dress. She'd been happy in dusty jeans and shirts. That crazy safari sunhat.

There'd only been one moment when she'd worn a dress. When he'd presented her with a cream concoction of delicate lace and silk that he'd seen in a shop window and hadn't been able to resist. As dresses went, it hadn't been sophisticated at all, but Julia had put it on and paraded in front of him as shyly as a new bride. It had been the first and only time she'd worn a dress, and that had been the night that he'd realised just how deeply—Kaden shut the door on that unwanted thought that had come out of nowhere. His insides clenched so hard he could feel them cramp.

Breathing deep, he brought his focus back to the here and now. To the woman by his side who was blissfully unaware of his wayward thoughts. He was vitally aware of the smooth curve of Julia's bare back in the dress. The pale luminescence of her skin. And the vulnerable part of her neck, which was revealed thanks to her upswept hair.

The dim hum of the conversation of hundreds of people reached them as they rounded a corner. Kaden took Julia's arm in his hand and felt her tension. Good. He wanted her to be tense. And unsettled. And all the things he was. They walked across a wide open-air courtyard and pristine Hussein servants dressed all in white opened huge doors into the glorious main ballroom.

Julia had been in plenty of stately homes and castles on her travels, but this took her breath away. She'd never seen such opulence and wealth. The huge ballroom was astounding, with an enormous domed ceiling covered in murals, and immense columns which opened out onto the warm, evocatively dusky night.

Waiting to greet them were the Sultan and his new bride—Kaden's sister Samia. As they approached, Julia saw Samia's face light up at seeing Kaden. She'd blossomed from a painfully shy teenager into a beauty with great poise. She'd always had a strong bond with her older brother, being his only full sibling, daughter of their father's first beloved wife. Their father had married again, and Julia remembered Kaden's stepmother as a cold, disapproving woman. She'd gone on to have three daughters of her own, but no sons which, Kaden had once told Julia, made her extremely bitter and jealous of Kaden and Samia. Certainly Julia could remember avoiding her malevolent presence at all costs.

Samia transferred her look to her then, and Julia attempted a weak smile. Samia looked at her with a mixture of bewilderment and hostility. It confused Julia, because she'd imagined that Kaden's younger sister would barely remember her.

But she didn't have time to analyse it. Kaden gripped

her hand, and after a few perfunctory words dragged her into the throng. Still shaken by Samia's reaction, Julia asked, "Why did Samia look at me like that? I'm surprised she even recognised me."

Kaden sent her a dark glance that was impossible to comprehend and didn't answer. Instead he took two glasses of champagne from a passing waiter and handed her one. Raising his glass in a mocking salute, he said, "Here's to us."

He clinked his glass to Julia's and drank deeply. She couldn't stop an awful hollow feeing from spreading through her whole body. She sensed that he was regretting having brought her here. No doubt he would prefer the balm of a woman well versed in the ways of being a compliant and beautiful mistress. Suitably appreciative of all he had to offer. All Julia wanted to do was to get out of there and curl up somewhere comforting and safe.

Several people lined up then, to talk to Kaden, and Julia became little more than an accessory while they fawned and complimented him on the news that the vast Burquati oil fields were to be drilled. Once again Julia had a sense of how much had changed for Kaden since she'd known him.

Before long the crowd were trickling into another huge banquet room for dinner, and she and Kaden followed. He was deep in conversation with another man, speaking French.

During the interminable dinner Julia caught Samia's eyes a few times, and still couldn't understand the accusing look. Kaden was resolutely turned away from her, talking to the person on his other side, which left Julia trying to conduct a very awkward conversation with the man on her left, who was infinitely more interested in her cleavage and had not a word of English.

Kaden was acutely aware of Julia, and how close her thigh was to his under the table. He had to clench his fist to stop himself from reaching out and touching it, resting his hand at the apex of her thighs, where he could feel her heat.

He felt constricted. His chest was tight. It had been ever since he'd seen Samia's reaction to Julia. Samia was the chink in his armour. She was the only one who knew the dark place he'd gone to when Julia had left Burquat. It made him intensely uncomfortable to remember it. He reassured himself now, as he had then, that it had only been because he'd physically ached for her, his lust unquenched.

He knew he shouldn't be ignoring Julia like this. It was unconscionably rude. But he was actually afraid that if she looked at him she'd see something that he couldn't guard in his eyes. Samia's reaction had been like rubbing sandpaper over a wound, surprising in its vividness.

Assuring himself that it was nothing—just another trick of the mind where Julia was concerned—Kaden finally gave up trying to pretend to be interested in what his companion was saying, made an excuse, and resolutely ignored Samia's pointed looks in his direction. They were like little lashes of a whip.

He turned to Julia and could see from the line of her back that she was tense, that her jaw was gritted. Instinctively he put his hand around the back of her neck, and felt her tense even more in reaction. He moved his fingers in a massaging movement and she started to relax. Kaden had to hold back a smile at the way he sensed she resented it.

Immediately a sense of calm and peace washed over Kaden, and for once he didn't castigate himself or deny it. He gave himself up to it. The rawness subsided.

After what felt like an interminable moment Julia finally turned to look at him, and as his gaze met hers his body responded with predictable swiftness.

"Kaden…?"

He looked at her, and in that moment some indecipherable communication seemed to flow between them. Her eyes were huge, swirling with emotion, and Kaden couldn't find the will to disguise his own response. The room faded and the din of conversation became silent.

Julia wanted to ask Kaden to stop looking at her like that…as if they were nineteen again and he wanted to discover the secrets of her soul. But she couldn't open her mouth. She didn't want to break the moment.

The clatter of coffee and liqueurs being served finally seemed to break through the trancelike state, and in an abrupt move Kaden took his hand off her neck, reached for her hand and stood up.

Julia gasped and looked around. A couple of people had started to drift away from the table, but many still sat. Kaden tugged at her and she had no choice but to stand. People were looking.

"Kaden…what are you doing? It's not over yet."

His eyes were so black Julia felt as if she might drown in them for ever.

"It is for us. I can't sit beside you for another minute and not touch you."

And with that he pulled her in his wake as he strode away from the table. Before she knew what was happening they were outside the ballroom. She could barely atch her breath, and when she stumbled a little he turned and lifted her into his arms.

"Kaden!" she spluttered, as they passed servants who looked away diplomatically, as if they were used to seeing such occurrences all the time.

She couldn't deny the thrill of excitement firing up her blood. Kaden was acting like a marauding pirate. He carried her all the way back through a labyrinthine set of corridors to their room, and only once inside the door, which he kicked shut with his foot, did he let her down. He wasn't even breathing heavily. But Julia was, after being carried so close to his hard-muscled chest.

In the bedroom, he let her down on shaky legs. He pushed her up against the firmly shut door, crowding her against it and saying, "We'll have to endure enough pomp and ceremony over the next two days, but every spare minute will be spent in this room. *That's* the focus of this weekend."

The sheer carnality stamped on his face and the hint of desperation in his voice stopped Julia from thinking too deeply about the hurt that lanced her—as if for a moment there, when he'd been looking at her at the table, she'd got lost in a fantasy of things being different.

And then his urgency flowed through to her—the realisation that even now time was slipping out of their hands. Overcome with an emotion she refused to look at, she took his face in her hands and for the first time felt somewhat in control. Kaden was right. Focus on the now, the physical. Not on the past. Or on a future that would never exist.

"Well, what are you waiting for, then?" And she kissed him.

* * *

Some hours later, Kaden was standing by the open French doors of the bedroom. B'harani lay before him like a twinkling carpet of gems. Soaring minarets nestled alongside modern buildings, and he knew that this was what he wanted to create in Burquat too. He'd already started, but he had a long way to go.

He sighed deeply and glanced back at the woman asleep in the bed amongst tumbled sheets. She was on her back, the sheet barely covering her sex, breasts bare, arms flung out, cheeks flushed. Even now his body hardened in helpless response. He grimaced. He'd taken her up against the door, her legs wrapped around his waist, with no more finesse than a rutting animal. And yet she'd met him every step of the way, her body accepting him and spurring him to heights he'd not attained in years.

Since her.

It all came back to her—as if some sort of circle was in effect, bringing them helplessly back to the beginning and onwards like an unstoppable force.

Julia woke slowly, through layers and layers of sleep and delicious lethargy. With an effort she opened her eyes and saw the tall, formidable shape of Kaden leaning against the open doors which led out to a private terrace. He was looking at her steadily, no expression on his face.

Helpless emotion bubbled up within her—especially when she saw the vast star-filled Arabian sky behind him. She had so much she wanted to say, but the past was all around her, in her. The lines were blurring ominously.

Instinctively she put out a hand and said huskily, "Kaden…"

For a long moment he just stood there, arms crossed, trousers slung low on narrow hips, top button open. He was so beautiful. And then he gritted out, "Damn you, Julia."

He strode back into the room, all but ripped off his clothes and came down over her like an avenging dark angel. All the inarticulate words she wanted to say were stifled by Kaden's expert touch and quickly forgotten.

When Julia woke on Sunday morning she ached all over. But it was delicious. Kaden was not there, and she found a note on his pillow to inform her that he'd gone riding.

When she thought of how Samia had been looking at her for the past two days she felt guilty, and she had no idea why.

The previous day, evening and night had passed in a dizzying array of events and functions all leading up to the grand ceremony today, which would be held in front of hundreds of guests and the media.

With a sigh Julia got up, went to the bathroom and stepped into the shower. Once finished, and dressed in a robe with a towel around her damp hair, she stepped out onto the open terrace to see that breakfast had been left for her on a table. She grimaced at the dewy fresh rose in an exquisite glass vase. That was a touch Kaden wouldn't welcome.

All that existed between her and Kaden was this intense heat. They couldn't even seem to hold a coherent conversation before things became physical. And she didn't doubt that was exactly how Kaden wanted it.

Julia assured herself stoutly that that was just fine. She picked up a croissant and walked to the wall, from where she could see the stunning city of B'harani spread out before her.

Her heart swelled—not for this city in particular, but for this part of the world. If any city held her heart it was Burquat, high on its huge hill, with its ancient, dusty winding streets and mysterious souks. But the air here was similar, and the heat…

She heard a sound behind her and turned to see Kaden standing at the doors. Her heart leapt. He was dressed in faded jeans which clung to powerful thighs and a sweaty polo shirt, boots to his knees. Damp hair stuck to his forehead.

As she watched, he started to pull off his shirt with such sexy grace that she dropped the croissant and didn't even notice. How could she feel so wanton and hot, mere hours after—?

Kaden threw down his top and came to Julia, hemming her in against the wall with his arms. His mouth found and nuzzled her neck. He smelled of sweat and musk and sex.

Julia groaned and said, half despairingly, "Kaden…"

He pulled one shoulder of her robe down and kissed her damp skin. "You missed a bit here…I think we need to remedy that."

With that awesome strength he picked her up, and within minutes they were naked and in the shower.

Much later, when the daylight was tipping into dusk outside, Julia woke from a fitful sleep. She felt disorientated and a little dizzy, even though she was lying down. Flashes of the day came into her head: the lavish wedding ceremony in the ornate ceremonial hall, Samia looking pale and so young, her husband tall and dark and austere, reminding Julia of Kaden.

And then, after a token appearance at the celebration, Kaden pulling her away, bringing her back here, where once again passion had overtaken everything. Her body was still sensitive, so she couldn't have slept for long.

She heard a noise and turned her head to see Kaden sitting at a table in the corner of the palatial room, with his slim laptop open in front of him. That lock of hair was over his forehead, and he sipped from a cup of what she guessed was coffee.

There was something so domestic about the scene that Julia's heart lurched painfully. And she knew right then with painful clarity that she had to be one to walk away this time. She couldn't bear to stand before Kaden again and have him tell her it was over.

As if he could hear her thinking, he looked over. He was already half dressed, in black pants and a white shirt. His look was cool enough to make her shiver slightly, and he glanced at his watch. "We have to be ready in half an hour for the final banquet."

Julia shot up in the bed, clutching the sheet. "You should have woken me." With dismay she thought of her dress for this evening that was already in the wardrobe. It was another couture gown, and she was going to require time to repair the damage and restore herself to something approximating normality. If she could ever feel normal again.

Feeling absurdly grumpy, Julia marched into the bathroom and locked the door behind her.

Kaden sat back in the chair and frowned, looking at the tangled sheets of the bed. The truth was he'd felt so comfortable here in the room, with Julia sleeping in the bed just feet away, that he'd forgotten all about waking her. His skin prickled at that. He'd felt that way before… with her, but never with another woman. Even with his own wife he'd insisted on separate bedrooms and living quarters. He knew now that if the situation had been reversed and he'd been married to Julia it would have been anathema not to share space with her.

If he'd married Julia.

That all too disturbing thought drove him up out of his chair and to the phone. He picked it up and gave instructions to the person on the other end.

When Julia emerged from the bathroom there was a pretty young girl dressed all in white waiting for her. She said shyly, "My name is Nita. I'm here to help you get changed."

Too bemused even to wonder where Kaden had disappeared to, Julia let Nita help her, and within half an hour she was dressed and ready again. At precisely that moment Kaden reappeared at the bedroom door, resplendent in another tuxedo. He held out his arm for Julia, who took it silently.

This time her dress was a deep purple colour. A tightly ruched strapless bodice gave way to swirling floor-length silk which was covered in tiny crystals. The effect was like a shimmering cloud as Julia walked alongside Kaden.

She could feel the ever-present tension in his form beside her, and marvelled at the irony of the whole situation. She was arguably living every little girl's fantasy, here in this fairytale castle, yet with the bleakest of adult twists.

She had to end this tonight—before he did. Before he could see how helplessly entangled she'd already become again.

A few hours later, when the crowd had watched Sultan Sadiq lead his new wife from the ceremonial ballroom, Julia was exhausted, and more than relieved when Kaden took her hand to lead her from the room. Her traitorous blood was humming in anticipation as they neared the bedroom. But she forced ice into her veins.

When they reached the room she extricated her hand and went and stood apart from him. He was surveying her warily, and she realised just how little they'd really communicated all weekend—as if he had been deliberately trying to avoid any conversation or any kind of intimacy beyond sex. It galvanised her.

She hitched up her chin. "The couple I was talking to earlier are leaving Burquat tonight, on a private flight back to England. They've offered me a seat on the plane if I'm ready to go in an hour."

Julia was vaguely aware of tension coming into Kaden's form. "You can't wait until tomorrow morning, when I am going to take you home?"

She shook her head, almost dizzy with relief that she was taking control of things. That Kaden wasn't coming closer, scrambling her brain. "There's no need. I need to get back. I've got work this week. I've got a life, Kaden. I think it's best if we just say this is over, here and now. What's the point in dragging it out?"

Kaden was seeing a red mist over his vision. So many conflicting things were hitting him at once. No woman had ever walked away from him, for one thing. But a dented ego had never been his concern. It was Julia, standing there so poised and cool, as if ice wouldn't melt in her mouth. When only hours before she'd been raking his back with her nails and sobbing for him to release her from exquisite pleasure.

Jerkily Julia moved to the drawers and picked up what looked like a jewellery box. She was already gathering her things to start packing. Filled with something that felt scarily close to panic, Kaden took a step forward and noticed how skittishly she moved back. Her face had an incredibly vulnerable expression but he blocked it out, and it was only then that he noticed—at the same time as she did—that some jewellery had fallen from the box after her skittish move.

He watched as she bent to pick up the trinkets and then, as if in slow motion, something gold fell back to the floor. Before he even knew what he was doing he'd stepped forward and picked the piece up.

Julia stood up. Her heart had stopped beating. It was like watching a car crash in slow motion. Kaden straightened. The distinctive gold chain with its detail of a love-knot looked ridiculously delicate in his huge hand. He didn't even look at her.

"You still have it."

Julia didn't have the strength to berate herself for having brought it. She swallowed and said, far more huskily than she would have liked, "Yes, I still have it."

Even now her fingers itched to touch the tell—tale spot where it usually sat, and she clenched her hand into a fist. Kaden looked at her and his face was unreadable, those black eyes like fathomless wells.

"You always touch your throat…" He reached out his other hand and touched the base of her neck with a long finger. "Just here…"

Julia gulped, and could see his eyes track the movement. With dread in her veins and a tide of crimson rising upwards she could only stand still as Kaden carefully stepped closer and opened the necklace, placing it around her neck and closing it as deftly as he had the day he'd bought it for her.

She felt the weight of the knot settle into its familiar place, just below the hollow at her throat. Kaden took his hands away, but didn't move back. Julia couldn't meet his eyes. Mortified and horrifically exposed.

Kaden looked at it for a long moment, and then he stepped back. When she raised her eyes to his they were blacker than she'd ever seen them. His face was set in stark lines. "If you're sure you want to go home now, I'll see that Nita comes to help you."

Julia shook her head, feeling numb. She wasn't sure how to take Kaden's abrupt *volte face*, when moments ago he'd looked as if he was about to tip her back onto the bed and persuade her to stay in a very carnal way. Now he looked positively repulsed. It had to be the necklace. He was horrified that she still had it, and what that might mean. Memories, the sting of rejection—all rushed back.

"It's fine. I don't need help."

Kaden saw Julia's mouth move but didn't really hear what she was saying. All he could hear was a dull roaring in his head, the precursor to a pounding headache. And all he could see was that necklace. It seemed to be mocking him. He could still feel its imprint on his hand.

A tightness was spreading in his chest. He had to get out of there *now*. He backed away from Julia. Gathering force within him was the overwhelming sensation of sliding down a slippery slope with nothing to hold onto.

Julia watched the play of indecipherable expressions cross Kaden's face. She felt like going over and thumping him. She wanted to wring some sort of response out of him… But then she felt deflated. How could she wring a response out of someone who had no feelings?

She swallowed painfully. "I… It's been—"

She stopped as he cut her off. "Yes," he agreed grimly. "It has. Goodbye, Julia."

And with that he turned and was gone, and all Julia's flimsy control shattered at her feet—because she felt as if she'd just been rejected all over again.

Less than an hour later Kaden was in his own private plane, heading back to Burquat. He'd actually had a meeting lined up the following morning, with some of Sultan Sadiq's mining advisors, but had postponed it. The fact was he'd felt an overwhelming need to get as far away from B'harani as possible, as quickly as possible.

He looked down at his hand. It was actually shaking. All he could see, though, was that necklace, sitting in his hand, and then around Julia's neck. It was obviously the necklace she went to touch all the time. It hung in exactly that spot, and when he'd put it on she'd looked *guilty*.

The question was too incendiary to contemplate, but he couldn't help it: who would keep and wear a cheap gold necklace for twelve years? It was the only piece of jewellery, apart from his ex-wife's wedding rings, that he'd ever given to a woman, and he remembered the moment as if it was yesterday.

Kaden's mind shut down… He couldn't handle the implications of this.

He watched the B'harani desert roll out below him,

and instead of feeling a sense of peace he felt incredibly restless. His hands clenched to fists on his thighs, he didn't even see the air hostess take one look at his face and beat a hasty retreat.

Kaden assured himself that for the first time since he'd met Julia he was finally doing the right thing. Leaving her behind in his past. Where she belonged.

CHAPTER SEVEN

"YOU are definitely pregnant, Julia. And if the dates you've told me are correct I'd say you're almost three months gone—at the end of your first trimester."

Julia's kindly maternal doctor looked at her over her half-moon glasses,

"Why didn't you come to me sooner? You must have suspected something, and we both know your periods are like clockwork."

Julia barely heard her. Shock was like a wall between her and the words. Of course she'd suspected something for the last two months, but she'd buried her head in the sand and told herself that fate couldn't be so cruel—not after years of trying for a baby with her husband. Hence the reason why her doctor knew her so well.

But then the problem hadn't been on her side. It had been her husband's.

The doctor was looking at Julia expectantly, and she forced herself to focus. "I just… I couldn't believe what it might be."

Her doctor smiled wryly. "Well it's a baby, due in about six months if all goes well." She continued gently, "I take it that as you're divorced the father is…?"

"Not my ex-husband, no." Julia bit her lip. "The father

is someone I once knew, long ago. We met again recently…"

"Are you going to tell him?"

Julia looked at her friend. "To be honest? I don't know yet…what I'm going to do."

The doctor's manner became more brisk. "Well, look, first things first. I'll book you in for a scan, just to make sure everything is progressing normally, and then we can take it from there— OK?"

One month later

Kaden paced in his office. The ever-present simmering emotions he'd been suppressing for about four months were threatening to erupt. Julia was here. Outside his office. Right now. She'd been waiting for over an hour. He would never normally keep anyone waiting that long but it was *Julia*, and she was here.

He ran a hand through his hair impatiently. What the hell did she want? His heart beat fast. Did she want to continue the affair? Had she spent the last months waking in the middle of the night too? Aching all over? He felt clammy. Would she be wearing that necklace?

He clenched a fist. Dammit. He'd hoped that by now he'd have chosen a wife and be in the middle of wedding preparations, but despite his aides' best efforts every potential candidate he'd met had had something wrong with her. One was too forward, another too meek, too sullen, too avaricious, too fake… The list was endless.

And now he couldn't ignore the fact that Julia Somerton had come to Burquat, going unnoticed on the flight lists because of her married name. In Burquat all repeat visitors were noted. She'd made her way to the castle and now she was sitting outside his door.

His internal phone rang and he stalked to his desk to pick it up. His secretary said, "Sire, I'm sorry to bother you, but Dr Somerton is still here. I think you should see her now. I'm a little concerned—"

Kaden cut her off abruptly, "Send her in."

Julia finally got the nod from Kaden's secretary, who was dressed not in traditional garb, as everyone used to be when she'd been here last, but in a smart trouser suit, with a fashionable scarf covering her hair. She'd been solicitous and charming to Julia, but Julia had noticed her frequent and concerned looks and wondered if she really looked so tired and dusty.

Her flight from London had left at the crack of dawn, and the journey from Burquat airport in a bone-rattling taxi with no air-conditioning had left her feeling bruised and battered. Thankfully, though, the incessant morning sickness she'd been suffering from had finally abated in the last month, and she felt strong enough to make the journey. Physically at least. Mentally and emotionally was another story altogether.

She knew that she'd lost weight, thanks to the more or less constant morning sickness, and she was pale. She couldn't even drum up the energy to care too much. She wasn't coming here to seduce Kaden. When he'd said that clipped and cold goodbye in B'harani after seeing the necklace it couldn't have been more obvious that he'd been horrified. She'd watched his physical reaction and known that any desire had died a death there and then.

Julia stopped herself from touching her neck now, and reminded herself that the necklace was safely back in the UK. She stood up and walked to the door. The secretary had told her to leave her suitcase by her desk. Julia hadn't even booked into a hotel yet, but she'd worry about that after.

The door swung open and she took a deep breath and stepped into Kaden's office. The early evening sunlight was in her face, so as the door shut behind her all she could see was the formidable outline of Kaden's shape.

She put a hand up to shade her eyes and tried to ignore the wave of *déjà-vu* that almost threatened to knock her out. The last time she'd been in this room—

"To what do I owe the pleasure, Julia?"

So cool.

Julia forced herself to breathe deep and focus on getting the words out. "I came because I have to tell you something."

Kaden finally stepped forward and blocked the light, so now Julia could see him. She felt her breath stop at being faced with his sheer male beauty again. And also because he had a beard—albeit a small one. His hair was longer too. He looked altogether wild and untamed in traditional robes, and her heart took up an unsteady rhythm.

Stupidly she asked, "Why do you have a beard?"

He put up a hand to touch it, almost as if he'd forgotten about it, and bit out, "I've spent the last ten days in the desert, meeting Bedouin leaders and councils. It's a custom among them to let their beards grow, so whenever I go I do the same. I haven't had time to shave yet. I just got back this morning."

Julia found this unexpected image of him so compelling that her throat dried. He was intensely masculine anyway, but like this… Her blood grew hot even as she looked at him. And he was looking at *her* as if she'd just slithered out from under a rock.

He quirked a brow. "Surely you haven't come all this way to question me on my shaving habits?"

A wave of weakness came over her then, and Julia realised she hadn't eaten since a soggy breakfast on the plane—hours ago. She cursed herself. She had to be more careful. But in fact, whether fatigue or hunger, whatever it was created a welcome cushion of numbness around her.

She looked at Kaden again and willed herself to be strong, straightening her spine. "No, I've come for another reason. The truth is that I have some news, and it affects both of us." She continued in a rush, before she could lose her nerve. "I'm pregnant, Kaden. With your baby… Well, actually, the thing is, it's not just one baby. If it was I might not have come all this way. But you see, I'm almost four months pregnant with twins…and the thought of two babies was a bit much to deal with on my own…and I know I could have rung, but I tried a few times…but that's when you must have been away in the desert and I didn't want to leave a message…"

Kaden lifted a hand. He'd gone very still and pale beneath his tan. "Pregnant? Twins?"

Julia nodded, hating herself for babbling like that. She'd wanted to be ultra-calm and collected, but now she was in front of Kaden she felt as if she was nineteen again. She wanted to run into his chest and have him hold her—but that scenario was about as likely as a sudden snow shower inside the palace.

"You look like you've *lost* weight—not as if you're pregnant." He sounded almost accusing.

Julia stifled a slightly hysterical laugh when she

thought of the sizeable bump under her loose top. She was already wearing stretch-waisted jeans.

His hand dropped. His eyes narrowed. He looked even wilder now. "And you say these babies are mine?"

At that insulting insinuation Julia actually swayed on her feet. Kaden came around his desk so fast it made her feel even dizzier. She put out a hand, as if that could stop him.

"Do you really think I came all this way for the good of my health? Just to pass off some other man's babies as yours?" Her voice rang with bitterness. "Believe me, I've been actuely aware of the awful irony of this situation for months of sleepless nights now. One baby I could have coped with. I wasn't even sure if I was going to tell you. But two babies…"

Kaden's eyes raked her from head to toe. His lip practically curled. "I used protection."

Julia's chin went up. "There is a failure rate, and clearly it failed."

The enormity of what Julia was saying, and to whom hit her then like a ton weight. Two babies. Who would be unwanted and unloved by their father. It was so much the opposite of what she'd once dreamt of with this man that the pain lanced her like a sharp knife right through the heart.

Everything was becoming indistinct and awfully blurry. That numbness was spreading. But in the face of his overwhelmingly hostile response Julia had to assert her independence. She had a horror of him assuming she'd come for a hand-out.

Faintly, Julia tried to force oxygen to her brain and to be articulate. "These are your babies, Kaden, whether you like it or not. And now that I've told you I'll leave.

I don't expect anything from you. I just wanted you to know that they exist…or will exist in about five months, all being well."

She turned on her heel, but it seemed to take an awful long time—as if everything had gone into slow motion. And then, instead of getting closer to the door, she seemed to be moving further and further away. With a cry of dismay as black edges appeared on her peripheral vision, Julia felt herself falling down and down. Only faintly did she hear a stricken "*Julia*!" and feel something warm and strong cushion her back before the blackness sucked her down completely.

"Why is she taking so long to come round?" Kaden asked the wizened palace doctor impatiently. He didn't like the metallic taste of fear in his mouth. "Shouldn't we go straight to the hospital? I told you she's pregnant."

The doctor was unflappable and kept his fingers on Julia's wrist, checking her pulse. Kaden had laid her down on the couch in his office before bellowing for his secretary to call Dr Assan. She'd been so limp and lifeless, her cheeks paler than he'd ever seen, dark bruises under her eyes.

And he'd kept her waiting all that time—after a long journey. She was pregnant. His conscience stung him hard.

Dr Assan looked at Kaden pacing near to him. "We're just waiting for the paramedics to come and then she will be taken to the hospital for a full examination. But as far as I can tell she is fine—probably just tired and dehydrated. You said she flew from England today?"

"Yes—yes, I did," Kaden agreed irritably. He was used to things happening quickly, and even though it was only a couple of minutes since she'd collapsed time seemed to have slowed down to the pace of a snail.

With a granite-like weight in his chest, he cursed himself for lashing out just now and insinuating that he might not be the father. Of *course* he believed her when she said the babies were his. She'd looked shell-shocked, not avaricious. He knew with a bone-deep certainty that she wasn't mercenary enough to make a false claim of paternity.

In five months' time he would have a ready-made family.

The thought was overwhelming.

Just then a knock came to the door, and in the flurry of activity Kaden concentrated on what they were doing to Julia. When they produced a stretcher to carry her out to the ambulance Kaden reacted to a surge of something primal, and waded in and picked her up into his arms himself, ignoring the paramedics.

Dr Assan motioned for them to follow Kaden as he strode out with Julia in his arms. Kaden was oblivious to the sea of people hurrying after him. He was only aware of the swell of Julia's pregnant belly against his chest, and something powerful rose up within him. His gut clenched tight. In his arms Julia stirred, but he didn't even break his stride as he looked down to see those pools of grey on him. Dazed and confused.

For a moment he forgot everything and reacted only to those eyes, and to the sensation of relief rushing through him. "Don't worry, you're safe, and I'm going to take care of you."

Julia was warm and secure in a dark place. But someone kept prodding her and shining a light in her eyes.

Instinctively she moved away from the light, but it kept following her until eventually she opened her eyes, and then it blinded her. She squeezed her eyes shut again, but heard a kindly voice saying, "Julia, you need to wake up now. You've given us all quite a fright."

In her hazy consciousness she heard an echo of Kaden's voice. *Don't worry...I'm going to take care of you...*

Without really knowing where she was or what was happening, she spoke from a place of urgent instinctive need, "Kaden…where is Kaden?"

A moment of silence, and then she felt his presence. A hand on hers. The relief was overwhelming. "I'm right here."

And at his touch and his voice it all came back. She wasn't nineteen any more. She was thirty-two, and pregnant with his babies. And he didn't want her—or them. Instantly she was cold and wide awake. Her eyes opened to see Kaden towering over her where she lay in a hospital bed, austere and remote in his robes and with that beard. She pulled her hand away, knowing that he must be hating her so much right now.

She looked to the man who had to be the doctor. "What happened?"

"You're severely dehydrated and fatigued. You'll need to be supervised on a drip for at least twenty-four hours. But apart from that everything is fine, and your babies are fine too. You just need rest and sustenance."

Julia immediately put a hand to the swell of her stomach and felt Kaden take a step back from the bed. She couldn't bear to look at him and see the censure in his eyes. The disgust he must feel that she was here, with this unwelcome news. The last woman in the world he would have picked to be the mother of his children.

She wondered again if she should have come, and her own doctor's words came back to her. "Julia, twins are a monumental task for anyone to take on board. You should not do this by yourself. You *must* include the father."

Kaden's doctor patted her hand and said, "I'll leave you alone now to rest."

He left the room and the silence was oppressive. Kaden walked around so that he was in Julia's line of vision. She felt acutely vulnerable, lying on the bed in a hospital robe.

"Where are my things?" she asked, as if that would postpone the painful conversation that was due.

"Your bag is still with my secretary and your clothes are here."

Julia bit her lip. "I can't believe I collapsed like that. I had no idea—"

He exploded. "How could you not have known you were so weak and dehydrated? For God's sake, you're pregnant. Are you not taking care of yourself?"

Julia could actually feel any colour she'd regained drain from her face. She'd known Kaden must be angry, but to see it like this….

He cursed and ran a hand through his unkempt hair. Somehow it only had the effect of making him look even more gorgeous. His black eyes came back to her, and to Julia's utter shock he looked contrite.

"I'm sorry. I had no right to speak to you like that. This has all been a bit of a shock…to say the least."

Julia's heart thumped. "I'm sorry that I couldn't warn you first. It just seemed too huge to send via text…" She blushed. "I don't even have your mobile number…and I didn't think it appropriate to leave a message with your aides."

His eyes narrowed on her face. "You said if it hadn't been twins you might not have told me?"

Julia avoided his eye guiltily, fingers plucking at the bedspread. "I don't know what I would have done, to be honest. It was pretty clear at our last meeting that neither one of us wanted to see each other again."

His mouth tightened. "Yes…but once a baby is involved…he or she…they are my heirs. Part of the royal Burquati dynasty. If you had kept my child from me I would never have forgiven you."

Julia looked at him, curling inwards at his censure. "I'm sure I would have told you about the baby, even though I know a lasting reminder of our…our meeting again was the last thing you wanted or expected."

Kaden's eyes flashed. For a long moment he didn't speak, and then he said, "That's beside the point now. We'll just have to make this work."

Julia's eyes narrowed on Kaden as a shiver of foreboding went down her spin. "What do you mean?"

"What I mean, Julia, is that we will be getting married. As soon as possible."

Kaden hadn't even realised he was thinking of such a thing until the words came out of his mouth, but to his utter surprise he felt a wave of equanimity wash over him for the first time in months.

Julia just looked at Kaden where he stood at the foot of the bed. Dominating. Powerful. Implacable. Inevitability and a sense of fatalism made her feel even weaker even as she protested shakily, "Don't be ridiculous, Kaden. We don't have to get married just because I'm having your baby."

He folded his arms, and corrected her. "*Babies*. And, yes, we do."

"But…" Julia's mind was feeling foggy again. She was glad she was lying down. "The people won't accept me as your wife…"

His mouth tightened. "They're conservative. It might take a while for them to accept you, but they will have no choice. You will be my sheikha—the mother of my children."

Julia wondered how it could be possible for her to feel dizzy when she was lying down, but the room was spinning and those black edges were creeping back. She heard Kaden swear again, and he moved towards her, but by the time he'd reached her she'd slipped back down into the comforting numbness of the black place.

One week later

"You are much improved, my dear. You should get out and enjoy some of the sunshine. Sit in the garden, breathe the fresh air. I'll go and get Jasmine to come and help you."

Julia smiled at the kindly Dr Assan and watched him leave. He'd been on standby since she'd returned to the palace from the hospital nearly four days before, and had been checking up on her at regular intervals.

For the last few days all she'd done was eat and sleep. And tried to block out Kaden's proposal—if she could even call it that. He hadn't mentioned it again. He'd come in and out of her bedroom and not said much at all, usually just looked at her broodingly.

Julia sighed deeply now and sat up. Her room was stupendously luxurious. Kaden had obviously had the palace redecorated in the intervening years, because before it had always had a very rustic and ascetic feel. Now, though, it might have come straight from the pages of an interior design magazine.

It hadn't completely lost that rustic feel. For instance it didn't share the de luxe opulence of the Hussein Castle in B'harani. But it was just as impressive. The palace itself looked as if it had been carved out of the hill it stood on, soaring majestically over the small city. Vast courtyards opened out into colourful gardens, where peacocks picked their way over glittering mosaics.

The interior stone floors were minimalist, but covered in the most exquisitely ornate rugs. The walls were largely bare, apart from the occasional silk wall hanging or flaming lantern. Windows were huge and open, with elaborate arches framing stunning views of the city.

Julia had a suite of rooms comprising a bedroom, bathroom and sitting room. With every mod-con and audio visual requirement cleverly tucked away so as not to ruin the authentic feel.

Outside the French doors of her sitting room lay a private courtyard filled with flowers. There was a pond, and a low wall which overlooked the ancient hilly city. In the near distance could be seen the blue line of the Persian Gulf. Seagulls wheeled over head, and the scent of the sea was never far away.

Julia felt incredibly emotional whenever she looked out over the city. From the moment she'd first come to Burquat the country and its people had resonated deep within her. She felt at home here. Or she had until that night—

"Dr Somerton? I'll help you get ready to go outside."

Julia glanced around from where she'd been sitting on the edge of the bed to see Jasmine, the pretty young girl who'd been helping her every day. She knew she'd only worry Dr Assan if she didn't go out, and she craved some air, so she smiled and let Jasmine help her.

Clothes had materialised one morning—beautiful kaftans and loose-fitting trousers to wear underneath—and Jasmine laid out a set now, in dark blue. They were comfortable and easy to wear in the heat—especially now that her bump seemed to be growing bigger by the day. It was as if her coming to Burquat had precipitated a growth spurt.

The palace had many gardens, but Julia's favourite so far was the orchard garden, filled with fruit-bearing trees. Branches were laden with plums and figs, and a river ran through the bottom of the garden, out of the palace grounds and down into the city. It was peaceful and idyllic.

Jasmine left her alone to walk there after showing her where a table and chair had been set up for her to rest in the shade. Julia couldn't believe how kind everyone was being to her. Certainly the oppressive atmosphere she remembered from Kaden's father's time had lifted, and she had to wonder if that was because Kaden's step-mother had also died, and some of the older, more austere aides were no longer part of Kaden's retinue.

She sat down and took a sip of fresh iced lemonade, savouring the tart, refreshing bite.

"I hope you don't mind if I join you."

It wasn't a question. Julia looked up to see Kaden standing nearby, and her belly automatically clenched. He'd shaved off his beard and had a haircut, but he looked no less wild or uncultivated despite the custom-made suit he now wore. He alternated between western and traditional dress easily.

She shook her head. As if by magic a man appeared with another chair, and through the trees some distance away Julia could see a man in a suit with an earpiece, watching over his precious Emir.

He sat down, his huge body dwarfing the chair, and helped himself to some lemonade. "You're looking much better."

Julia fought not to blush under Kaden's assessing gaze as it swept down over her body, and wished she'd put her hair up and some make—up on. Then she remembered how quick he'd been to let her go in B'harani and looked away, afraid he might see something of her emotions. Once again she felt humiliated heat rise at remembering that he'd seen the necklace.

"I'm feeling much better, thank you. All of your staff have been so kind. I should be well enough to return home soon. I'll have to organise a plane ticket back to the UK."

He shook his head. "You're not going home, Julia. I'm already arranging to have your belongings packed up and sent here. We can rent out your house in London while you decide what you want to do with it."

Julia looked at Kaden and her mouth opened. Nothing came out.

He leaned forward, his face grim. "We are getting married, Julia. Next week. Your life is here now—with me."

Panic bloomed in her gut, but it had more to do with the prospect of a lifetime facing Kaden's cool censure than the prospect of a lifetime as his wife. "You can't keep me here if I decide I want to go home. That would be kidnap."

"It won't be kidnap because you'll be staying of your own free will. You know it's the right thing to do."

Julia reacted. "Is it really the right thing to agree to a marriage just for convenience's sake?" She laughed a little wildly. "I've already been through one unhappy marriage. I'm not about to jump head-first into another one."

Kaden was intent, his face stark. "This isn't about just you—or me. It's about the two babies you are carrying. And it's about the fact that everyone knows you're here and that we were once lovers. The news of your pregnancy will soon filter out, and I want us to be married before that happens. For your sake and our babies' sakes as much as mine."

Our babies. Her eyes were wide. She felt control of her own existence slipping out of her grasp. She knew she must have gone pale again, but at least she felt stronger now.

As much as she didn't want to admit it, his words resonated within her on a practical level—bringing up two children on her own would be next to impossible with no familial support to speak of. Both her adoptive parents had died some years previously. Her divorce had wiped out any savings and a meagre inheritance. How could she afford childcare for two children unless she worked like a demon? And what kind of a life would that be for her children?

But Kaden's words also impacted on her at a much deeper and more visceral level. Growing up knowing she was adopted had bred within Julia an abiding need to create her own family. To have children and give them the assurance of their lineage and background that she'd never had. Her adoptive parents had loved her, of course… But she'd never really got over the stain of being unwanted by her birth mother and father. Irrationally she felt it was a reflection on *her*, something *she'd* done. And she had carried it down through the years to make what had happened with Kaden so much more devastating. But he was the last person she could confide in about this…

The haunting call of the *muezzin* started up in the city nearby and it tugged on her heart. She'd once fantasised about living here for ever with Kaden, but this was like a nightmare version of that dream.

As if sensing her turmoil, Kaden came out of his chair and down on one knee beside Julia. He took her hand in his. For a hysterical moment she thought he was going to propose to her, but then he said, "You said it yourself when you came here—two babies change everything. I won't allow them to be brought up on another continent when their heritage is here, in this country. It's *two* babies, Julia. How can you even hope to cope with that on your own? They deserve to have two parents, a secure home and grounding. I can provide that. They will have roles to fulfil in this country—one of them will be the next Emir, or Queen of Burquat. Who knows? They might even rule together…"

Julia moved back in her seat. The thought of him seeing how his touch affected her was terrifying. "They also deserve to have two parents who love one another."

Kaden's face became cynical as he dropped her hand and spat out, "*Love*? You speak of fairytales that don't exist. We will make this work, Julia, because we have to. We don't need love."

She saw the conflict in his eyes and on his face. His mouth was a thin line.

He stood up, instantly tall and intimidating. "I'll do whatever I have to to make this work. You know this is the only way. I will be a good husband to you, Julia. I will support you and respect you." A flash of heat sparked between them. "And I will be faithful to you."

A week later Julia looked at herself in the floor-length mirror in her dressing room. The dawn light hadn't even broken outside yet. According to Burquati tradition, they would exchange vows and rings in a simple civil ceremony as dawn broke.

At any other time Julia would have found the prospect impossibly romantic. As it was all she could think about was Kaden's grim avowal: "*I'll do whatever I have to to make this work.*"

She was wearing an ivory gown, long-sleeved and modest, but it clung to every curve and moved sinuously when she walked. Thankfully the heavy material skimmed over her bump, so it wasn't too glaringly obvious. A lace veil was pinned low on the back of her head, and Jasmine had coiled her hair into a loose chignon. She wore pearl drop earrings, and Kaden had presented her with a stunning princess cut diamond ring set in old gold the day before, telling her it had been his mother's engagement ring, to be kept for his own bride.

The thought of wearing a ring that his first wife had also worn made her feel sullied somehow, but she hadn't had the nerve to say anything to a closed-off and taciturn Kaden. It couldn't be clearer that he was viewing this marriage as a kind of penance.

If she was stronger… Julia sighed. It was more than

strength she needed to resist the will of Kaden. And deep within her she had to admit to a feeling of security at knowing that at least her babies would live lives free of shadows and doubts. She wasn't even going to admit to another much more personal and illicit feeling…of peace. Julia quickly diverted her thoughts away from *that* dangerous area.

She thought of the whirlwind it had been since she'd tacitly agreed to this marriage. And of the very muted fanfare that had greeted the public announcement a few days ago. At dinner on the evening their nuptials had been announced, Julia had voiced her building concern to Kaden; the reality of what might be expected of her had started sinking in. "Wasn't your mother half-English? The people will be used to a foreign Sheikha, won't they?"

Kaden had avoided Julia's eye, and that had made her instantly nervous. "Unfortunately the track record of Sheikhas here hasn't been good since my mother died. Both my wife and my stepmother never really connected with the people. As for my mother… They accepted her, yes…after a rocky start. The truth is that my father went against his own father's wishes to marry for love. The only reason he was allowed to marry my mother was because she came from a lineage on her father's side that went back as far as our own."

He'd looked at her then, with a carefully veiled expression. "It took the people some time to accept her, but they did, and when she died they were just as devastated as my father. He never came to terms with her death during Samia's childbirth. It changed him…made him withdraw and become more cynical… He blamed himself for having pursued his own selfish desires in bringing her here."

Julia had protested. "But it was just an awful tragedy."

Kaden had abruptly changed the conversation then.

Julia had hardly slept since that night, more and more aware of how hard it was likely to be for her to be accepted by the Burquati people, and wondering how far Kaden was prepared to test his people's limits of acceptance to keep his heirs safe—and here.

CHAPTER EIGHT

KADEN paced back and forth in the huge ceremonial ballroom of the palace. He was dressed in the royal Burquati military uniform. His chief aides and the officiator for the wedding ceremony waited patiently. He looked out of the window for the umpteenth time and saw the faint pink trails in the clear sky that heralded the dawn breaking. The thought of how delicate Julia had looked at dinner the previous evening. She'd hardly said a word, and her eyes had been huge, full of shadows, with the faintest purple smudges underneath.

He bit back a curse, hating the urgency rushing through his blood that had nothing to do with protocol and much to do with his disturbing need to see Julia.

He hadn't felt like this on his first wedding day. He'd been battling an almost dread feeling of suffocation that day. But since his marriage had ended he'd put that down to a presentiment of what had happened with his wife, and nothing to do with the lingering memory of another woman.

A sound came from the other end of the room and Kaden turned. His mind was emptied of all thought. Julia was a vision in ivory edged with pale gold as she walked towards him, with Jasmine holding her dress behind her. Her face was obscured by a long veil, and his eyes dropped to where the swell of her belly told the story of why they were getting married.

Something so fierce and primal gripped him in that moment that he had to clench his jaw and fists to stop shaking with it as Julia came to a stop just inches away. She was looking down, and Kaden longed to tell everyone to leave so that he could pull back the veil and tip her face up to his.

Instead he reached for her hand and lifted it up, bringing it to his mouth. Her head lifted and he could see the shape of her face, the flash of grey eyes, as he kissed her palm. Her perfume was soft and delicate, winding around him like a silken tie, bringing with it evocative memories and whispers of the past.

In that moment he hated her for coming back into his life, for reawakening a part of himself that he'd thought buried for ever. The only part of him that had ever been vulnerable, and the only part of him that had believed a different future was possible for him. It hadn't been.

With Julia's hand still in his he turned to the officiator and said curtly, "Let's get started."

What felt like aeons later Julia was sitting beside Kaden at the massive dining table and her face felt as if it was frozen in a rictus grin. Her heart hurt. From the moment Kaden had said, "*Let's get started*" earlier, he'd been curt to the point of dismissal.

She dreaded to think what the photographs would look like—Kaden tall and stern, and her like a rabbit in the headlights. Only a few of months ago she'd been independent and strong, living her life, and now she'd morphed into someone she barely recognised. All because of this man coming back into her life like a tornado.

A small voice mocked her: *she'd been with him every step of the way.*

Julia straightened her spine. She wasn't going to let Kaden ignore her like this. She turned towards him, where he sat beside her. He was looking out over the sea of some five hundred guests with a brooding expression. She knew none of them except for his three youngest sisters, who had travelled from their schools and colleges for the weekend. Samia and her husband had been unable to attend, and Julia had felt a little relieved, not sure if she could take Samia's hostility again.

"Kaden?"

He turned, and Julia sucked in a shocked breath when she saw the look of pure bleakness on his face. But in an instant it was gone, and replaced with something she thought she'd never see again. *Heat.* He took one of her hands and brought it to his mouth. His touch sent her pulse skyrocketing and a flood of heat between her legs.

She tried to pull her hand back, seriously confused, forgetting what she'd wanted to say in the first place. "Kaden…?"

"Yes, *habiba*?

She felt very shaky all of a sudden. "Why are you looking at me like that?"

He arched a brow. "Is this not how a man is supposed to look at his wife?"

Feeling sickened, Julia wrenched her hand free from his. He was faking it. Of course. In front of his guests.

Julia muttered something about the bathroom and got up, barely noticing Kaden's frowning look as she hurried away, head down.

Kaden watched Julia walk away, eyes glued to the graceful lines of her body in the stunning dress. The veil was long gone, and her hair was coiled at the nape of her neck. She was like a warmly glowing pearl against this backdrop. And for a moment, before she'd called him, he'd been drawn back into the memory of their time in the desert just before everything had changed.

He'd once dreamed of exactly this moment—having Julia by his side as his Queen, his heart full to bursting with pride and love… And then she'd called his name and he'd realised that it wasn't like the dream. That dream had existed in the mind of a foolishly romantic young man who hadn't known any better. *This* was reality, and reality was a long way from any dream.

Cursing himself, he could still feel desire like a tight coil in his body. A desire he'd curbed for too long. Kaden threw down his napkin and stood up. They'd had speeches and ceremonial toasts. Everyone now expected the Emir to take his leave with his wife. Striding out of the room, servants scurrying in his wake, Kaden felt his blood growing hotter by the second.

Julia had made her way out of the crowded room feeling stifled and extremely emotional. Jasmine had appeared as if from nowhere to guide her back to her rooms. She still didn't even know her own way around the palace!

When Jasmine showed her into the suite it took a minute before she realised that the distinctively masculine furnishings weren't familiar. She turned to Jasmine, who was waiting patiently for instructions.

"These aren't my rooms."

Jasmine inclined her head deferentially. "Sheikh

Kaden told me to move your things in here. You will be sharing his rooms from now on."

Julia's heart fluttered in her chest. She wasn't sure what Kaden was playing at, but she told Jasmine she wouldn't need her further. When the girl had left, emotion started rising again, and blindly Julia made her way out to Kaden's outdoor terrace. Much grander than her own.

It was dusk, and the call of an exotic bird pierced the air as Julia gripped the wall and looked out over Burquat. She could see people coming and going about their business far below, a line of blue which indicated the sea. She smelled the tang of salty air.

And all Julia could think of was how far Kaden was willing to go to make sure everyone believed he desired his wife, and how the immense crowd of guests had looked at her warily, with few smiles. An overwhelming feeling of aloneness washed over her. She put a hand to her bump and thought of her babies. *They* would be protected from this awful feeling of isolation. But she couldn't help, for one weak and self—indulgent moment, feeling sorry for herself. And she couldn't help the tears springing into her eyes and overflowing.

Kaden came into his rooms silently, and immediately saw Julia standing outside. The line of her back looked incredibly slim and tense, and the coil of her hair was shining in the dusky light. A curious feeling of peace mixed with desire rushed through his veins.

He moved forward and saw that Julia heard him. She tensed even more, and didn't turn around. Irritation prickled over his skin. "Julia?"

Julia was frantically swallowing and trying to blink back tears, her cheeks stinging. The thought of Kaden witnessing her turmoil was too much, but she heard him come closer, and then his hands came onto her shoulders and he was turning her around.

She looked down in a desperate bid to hide, but he tipped her chin up. She looked at him almost defiantly through the sheen of tears. He frowned, eyes roving over her face. "You're crying."

Kaden was not prepared for the blow he felt to his solar plexus. Julia's face was pale and blotchy, wet with tears. Eyes swimming, dark pools of grey. Her mouth trembling.

"It's nothing," she said huskily, lifting a hand to wipe at her cheek.

Kaden took her hand away and cupped her face. His chest felt so constricted he could hardly breathe. His thumbs wiped away the lingering tears.

"What is it?"

Julia bit her lip, clearly fighting for control. "It's just all…a bit much. Finding out about my pregnancy, coming here…my life changing overnight."

A solid mass of something dark settled into Kaden's chest. Clearly this was not what she'd envisaged for herself. He felt the sting of guilt. He'd seduced her. And changed their lives.

"Julia…you will not want for anything ever again. You or our babies. You can be happy here."

She gave a half-strangled laugh. "When your people look at me as if I'm about to do something scandalous?"

He grimaced. "They just need time, that's all. There's been so much change in Burquat…my divorce…"

Julia was finding it hard to breathe with Kaden so close and holding her face. She couldn't bear for him to see her desire on top of this. She tried to pull his hands down but they were immovable. She looked into his eyes. "Kaden…it's OK. You don't have to pretend here. No one is watching. And I don't expect to share your rooms. I'll go back to my own."

"Pretend what?"

Julia avoided his gaze. "Pretend to…want me."

Kaden frowned. Pretend to want her? Could she not feel how on fire he was for her? And then the notion that perhaps she didn't want *him* sent something cold to his gut. He moved his hands and took her wrists. He could feel the hammering of her pulse. A sigh of relief went through him.

"Julia, look at me."

With obvious reluctance she lifted her head. Her eyes were clear now, but no less troubled.

"What on earth made you think that I didn't want you?"

Now she frowned, a flush coming into her cheeks. "That last night in B'harani…you were so quick to leave…" She stopped when she thought of his reaction to the necklace, and then said hurriedly, "Not that I wanted it to go on. I was happy for it to be over. But I just thought…"

"That I didn't desire you any more?"

She nodded, and Kaden moved close to her again, lifting her hands and trapping them against his chest, where she would feel the thundering beat of his heart. Standing so close to her like this was exquisite torture. A deep contentment flowed through him that he wasn't even aware of. He thought of the necklace then, of how seeing it had made him feel. But instead of dousing his desire, or making him want to flee, it actually made him feel even hotter.

Julia's cheeks flushed even more when Kaden moved so close that his erection pressed against her lower belly. Sensation exploded behind his eyes, through his body, and he had to bite back a groan. He said throatily, "Does that feel like the response of a man who doesn't desire you?"

He marvelled. How could she not know? He felt as if every time he looked at her she must see the extent of his hunger. She was so different from any other woman he'd known. He'd almost forgotten that a woman like her could exist, and had a fleeting image of how bleak his life would have been if he'd not met her again.

Julia's eyes dropped to Kaden's mouth. She was transfixed. Almost without realising what she was doing, she extricated her hand from his grip and reached up to trace the sensuous line of his lips.

Kaden's hand went around the back of her neck, under the heavy fall of her hair, massaging the tender skin and muscles. His other hand was on her waist, big and possessive. Her breathing was already coming quickly, and she was telling herself to try and stay clear…but it was impossible.

Kaden dropped his head to hers. They were so close now that his breath feathered along her mouth. "I've never wanted another woman the way I want you."

Julia looked into his eyes and saw the flame in their depths. She reached up and pressed her mouth to his softly, chastely. For a moment he did nothing, and then with an urgency that made her blood exult in her veins he brought her even closer and fused his mouth to hers, opening her up to him so that his tongue could explore and seek a deeper intimacy.

Julia's hands and arms wound around Kaden's neck,

fingers tangling in the silky hair brushing his collar. She could feel the swell of her belly pressing into him, the stab of his erection against her, and something deeply feminine and primal burned within her. This was *her* man.

Perhaps their desire was the one pure, true thing between them? Perhaps they could build on this? Perhaps one day the fact that he'd rejected her once would fade away?

All of these thoughts and other incoherent ones raced through her head in time with her heart, but she just wanted to lose herself in the release only he could give.

He drew back and took in a deep, ragged breath, eyes looking wild. Julia's mouth was burning.

"Wait… I want you so badly, Julia… But can we? I mean, is it safe?"

For a moment she didn't understand what he was saying, and then she felt him place a hand to her belly. Something inside her melted even more. Blushing, because she was aware of the rampant need inside her, she said, "Dr Assan told me that it would be OK if we wanted to…you know…"

Kaden clamped her face in his hands and said, "Thank God."

And then they were kissing again, and that helpless emotion was bubbling up within Julia. There was a desperation about their kiss, as if they'd been separated for years. As if something had broken open.

He broke the kiss only to lift her up into his arms and carry her into the dimly lit bedroom, with its huge king-size bed. Julia kept her eyes on Kaden, as if to look away might break the spell.

With a kind of reverence Kaden divested Julia of her

jewellery and started to take off her clothes, undoing her dress at the back so that it fell open and then down to the floor in a pool of silk and satin at her feet, heavy under its own weight.

She stood in her underwear with her head tipped forward as Kaden took the pins out of her hair so that it tumbled around her shoulders. She could feel him open her bra, and shivered deliciously when his finger traced the line of her spine all the way down to her buttocks. Her breasts were heavy, nipples tight and tingling.

Gently he turned her to face him again, and pulled the open bra down her arms and off. She felt self-conscious for a moment, aware of her bigger breasts and her rounded belly. But under Kaden's hot gaze all trepidation fled. He cupped her breasts, eyes dark and molten as he moved his thumbs over the taut peaks. They were more sensitive now, and Julia groaned softly. Her hands were shaking with need as she reached out to take off Kaden's jacket and shirt. The buttons were elaborate and proved too much for her clumsy ministrations.

Kaden took her hands away and she watched, dry-mouthed, as bit by bit his glorious torso was revealed. Stepping close, she pressed a kiss to one flat nipple, tugging gently with her teeth and then smoothing it with her tongue. Kaden's hand speared her hair, holding her head. Julia exulted in his rough breathing, in the way his chest filled to suck in more air.

Her hands had found his belt and buckle. Urgently she opened them and pushed his trousers and briefs down to the floor, freeing his impressive erection. Drawing back for a moment, she looked down, feeling dizzy with desire. She reached out a hand and touched him, stroking the hard length, feeling the decadent slide of silky skin over steel.

"Julia..."

Kaden sounded hoarse. Julia acted on pure instinct and bent her knees until she knelt before him on the floor. Still holding him, she took the tip of him into her mouth, tongue swirling around him. Fresh heat flooded through her at doing something so wanton, and she only dimly heard Kaden say harshly, "Stop... *God*, Julia, if you keep doing that I won't—"

She felt Kaden gently pull her head away. She looked up, and the feral, almost fierce expression on his face reminded her of a wild and beautiful animal. He pulled her to her feet. "You don't know what you do to me. I won't last...and I want you too much. I need to be inside you. *Now.*"

Within what felt like seconds they were on Kaden's bed, with not a stitch of clothing between them. Kaden's hands smoothed down over Julia's curves, her belly. She reached for him. "Kaden, I need you."

His hand dipped between her legs, feeling for himself that she was ready, and if Julia hadn't been so turned on she would have been embarrassed by the triumphant glitter in Kaden's eyes.

He settled his lean hips between her legs, one hand on her thigh, pushing it wider, careful not to rest his weight on her belly. Julia arched her back, nipples scraping against his chest.

And then, just when she was about to plead and beg, she felt him slide into her, inch by delicious inch, filling her and stretching her. Eyes wide, she looked at him as he started to thrust, taking them higher and higher.

Time was transcended. All that existed was this blissful union. And Julia was borne aloft on a wave of ecstasy so overpowering that it seemed to go on for ever, her whole body pulsing and clenching for long seconds even after Kaden's seed had spilled deep inside her. After a timeless moment he extricated himself and pulled her tight into his chest, arms wrapped around her. Julia wondered for one lucid moment before she fell asleep if this was a dream.

Kaden lay awake beside Julia. His heartbeat was still erratic, and a light sweat sheened his skin. Julia was curled into his chest, bottom tucked close into the cradle of his thighs. Already he was growing hard at the feel of her lush behind. Once again he was struck with the immutable truth that no other woman had this effect on him after making love. He felt all at once invincible, and yet more vulnerable than he'd ever felt.

One hand was on Julia's belly, his fingers spread across the firm swell. He put the feelings welling up inside him down to knowing that she was pregnant—with *his* babies, his seed. Undoubtedly that was what had imbued their lovemaking with a heightened intensity.

But as Kaden finally let sleep claim him his overriding feeling wasn't one of peace at being able to put the experience into a box. It was the same disconcerting one he'd had in B'harani, when he'd seen Julia wearing that necklace. He felt as if he was sliding down that slippery slope again, with nothing to hold onto, and there was a great black yawning abyss at the bottom, waiting to suck him down.

A few hours later, as dawn broke outside, Kaden woke sweating and clammy, his heart racing. He'd just had a vivid dream of nightmare proportions. He'd been surrounded by a crowd of faceless people and held back by hundreds of hands as he was forced to watch Julia make love to another man. He'd wanted to rip that man limb from limb. He felt nauseous even now, as it came back in lurid detail.

He looked to where Julia lay sleeping on her side on the other side of the bed and felt all at once like holding her close and running fast in the opposite direction.

Two weeks after that cataclysmic wedding night Julia was wondering if it had been a dream. It *felt* like a dream, because they hadn't made love since then. Kaden had been cool the following morning at breakfast, while Julia had felt as if she'd survived an earthquake.

He'd informed her, while barely meeting her eyes, "Unfortunately local elections are coming up this week, which means that we'll have to postpone a honeymoon."

Julia's insides had curdled in the face of this remote man. How could she have been seduced so easily into thinking she'd seen something of the young man she'd fallen in love with?

"That's fine with me," she'd answered stiffly. "I hadn't expected anything else."

And then he'd said, "I've arranged for you to have lessons in Burquati history and royal protocol. You'll be well prepared for any public engagements. I should be able to accompany you until you get your bearings. The lessons will give you a broad overview of everything you need to know, and some tuition in our language."

Now Kaden shifted on the other side of the dinner table, and Julia glanced up guiltily to see him assessing her. His eyes dropped to her hand.

"Why aren't you wearing your engagement ring?"

Julia looked at the plain gold wedding band on her finger and flushed. "I was afraid I might lose it."

She saw his sceptical look, and then felt a surge of adrenalin. The fact that he'd clearly been avoiding coming to bed until she was asleep for the past two weeks, while she lay there aching for him to touch her, was inciting hot anger.

She lifted her chin. "The truth is that I don't like the idea of wearing a ring that was given to your first wife."

"Why would you feel that?"

She frowned. "You said that it was your mother's ring, which was to be given to the woman you married… I just assumed—"

He cut her off. "I gave Amira a different ring—one that she kept when we were divorced…" His mouth tightened, "I believe it fetched a nice price at auction in London a few months ago. Clearly her generous divorce settlement is fast running out."

Julia was disconcerted, her anger fading. "Why didn't you give your mother's ring to her?"

Kaden looked at Julia, and those big grey eyes threatened him on so many levels. He shrugged nonchalantly, very aware that this was exposing him. He hadn't given the ring to Amira because it hadn't felt right. And yet with Julia there'd been no hesitation.

"It didn't suit her colouring. It meant nothing significant."

Julia was stung. Well, she'd got her answer. He'd given it to *her* because it suited her colouring. The fact that she hungered so desperately for him mocked her, when she knew more certainly than ever that the only reason she was here at all was because of the heirs she carried. He couldn't even bring himself to make love to her again.

Wanting to disguise how hurt and vulnerable that made her feel, she said, "How do I know that once I have these babies you won't try to extricate yourself from *me*? You cast your first wife out just because she couldn't give you an heir. Obviously you weren't committed enough to pursue other options. Perhaps it's just the heirs you care about? Maybe a wife is superfluous to your needs?"

Kaden's mouth tightened with anger. "For your information, I did all I could to make my marriage work. Amira was the one who insisted on a divorce, because she knew she could never give me an heir. She wouldn't even discuss options. And I'm still paying for ongoing treatment to get her over her phobia."

Julia felt deflated when she thought of the fact that if his wife had been more amenable they might still be married. Cheeks flaming, she said, "I'm sorry. I had no right to assume I knew what had happened. It must have been…very painful."

Kaden emitted a curt laugh. "I wasn't in love with her, Julia. It was an arranged marriage." His voice sounded surprisingly bitter. "She had the right lineage."

Julia glanced at him, pushing down the lancing pain at this evidence of his cynicism. "And now you've got the heirs, but a wife with all the wrong lineage."

He just looked at her with those black eyes, and for the first time Julia felt something rising up within her—something she couldn't keep suppressing.

She fiddled with her napkin and avoided Kaden's eye. "Speaking of lineage, there's something you should probably know." She rushed on before she could lose her nerve. "I'm adopted, Kaden. I was adopted at birth. I know who my birth mother is, but she doesn't want to know me. For all I know she could even be dead by now."

Julia was breathing fast, aghast that she'd just blurted out the stain on her soul like that.

Kaden said carefully, "Why did you never tell me this before?"

Julia shrugged minutely, still avoiding his eye. "I don't talk about it—ever."

"Why not? It's not a bad thing. Plenty of people are adopted. I would have considered adoption myself if Amira had been open to the idea."

Shock at Kaden's easy acceptance made her look up. His eyes were dark, assessing. Not cold and judgemental. Julia felt as if she was being drawn into those eyes. His reaction was loosening something that had always felt tight inside her.

"From the day my parents told me I was adopted, when I turned thirteen, I always felt…*less*." She grimaced. "My parents went out of their way to assure me they loved me, but to know that someone else had had you first…and let you go because they didn't want you…" Even now Julia shivered.

"What about your father? You say your birth mother didn't want to know you?"

"The records from the agency showed that my parents hadn't been married. I found out that my father had emigrated to Australia almost immediately after my birth. He was too far away to trace, so I focused on my mother. I was too impatient to write, so not long before I came here to work on the dig I tracked down her phone number and called her…"

Julia smiled tremulously. "She knew exactly who I was. It was as if she'd been waiting for my call." Her smile faded. "But then she just said, '*Don't call here again. I don't want to have anything to do with you. I gave you up once and it's done*'."

The pain in Julia's heart was acute. She only realised she was crying silent tears when Kaden took her hand across the table, enveloping her in warmth.

"It sounds to me as if giving you up was an incredibly traumatic experience for her. Perhaps it's something she simply couldn't deal with."

Julia brushed away the tears and attempted a smile. "I know… I saw a counsellor attached to the adoption agency before I contacted her, so I was warned about the reaction I might get. But somehow I'd hoped for the kind of thing you see in the movies—the great reunion. Stupid…"

Kaden was shaking his head, his hand tightening on hers. "Not stupid at all. It's very human. I'm sorry, Julia…really sorry you went through that. I can't imagine what it's like to grow up not knowing where you've come from."

Feeling very exposed and brittle at Kaden's sensitivity, Julia pulled her hand back from his and put it on her belly, saying lightly, "At least these little ones won't ever have to face that."

Kaden was grim. "No, they won't."

The evidence of Kaden's grimness made Julia's emotions see-saw all over the place. She desperately wanted him to hold her…to make love to her and help her forget her pain which was far too close to the surface. But he hadn't touched her in two weeks, and wasn't likely to any time soon.

In a bid to escape before he could see the extent of how this affected her, she stood up. "I'm quite tired this evening… If you'll excuse me…?"

Kaden stood too. "Don't forget about the visit to the new hospital wing tomorrow."

"Oh…"

Julia *had* forgotten about her first public function tomorrow. She was due to cut the ribbon on a new wing of the national hospital. Immediately her concerns about going out in public rose up.

Kaden said, "I'll be with you tomorrow. All you'll have to do is smile and wave. They won't expect any more. They'll just want to see you."

Julia turned to walk away from the table, but Kaden caught her wrist. She looked back. She could feel her pulse throbbing against his hand and flushed.

She took her wrist from his grip. After everything she'd just shared, the deep vulnerability she felt was acute enough to be a physical ache within her. She forced a smile. "I'll be fine. I'm looking forward to it."

She left the room, feeling Kaden's black eyes boring into her back.

Kaden waved away the staff that came in to clear the plates from the private and intimate dining room not far from their suite of rooms. He needed to be alone, to digest everything Julia had just told him. Suddenly restless, he stood up, his long robes falling around him.

He paced back and forth, as if that might dampen the ever-present burn of desire, made worse now after feeling Julia's hectic pulse. It was all jumbled up in his head: his need to lose himself in her body; his equal need to keep his distance; the almost overwhelming need to protect her from ever being hurt again as she so evidently had been by her birth mother.

Julia had looked so vulnerable just now, and he hated the thought of exposing her to the crowds tomorrow. But he couldn't avoid it. He felt inordinately protective, but told himself it was a natural response because she was pregnant, and not because of what she'd revealed about her birth.

He'd had no clue about her adoption. From what she'd told him about herself years before he'd guessed she came from a solidly middle class background. When she hadn't talked about family too much he'd just put it down to English reticence. The fact that she'd made that painful contact with her birth mother just before she'd come to Burquat was uncomfortable for him to dwell on.

For a second Kaden had a glimpse into how rudderless *he* might have felt if he hadn't grown up knowing exactly where he'd come from. The sliver of isolation that washed through him at contemplating that scenario made him want to call Julia back, so that he could hold her close and never let her go again.

He immediately rejected that urge. His hand clenched to a fist. *This* was what he'd been avoiding ever since their wedding night. This rising tide of emotions that he refused to look at or acknowledge. The depth of passion on that night had stunned him. And that awful dream… which had obviously been precipitated by sleeping with Julia. Perhaps here in Burquat the memories were too close to avoid.

The truth was that when Julia touched him he became something else—someone else. It was too reminiscent of how she'd made him feel before. He'd never forget that struggle with his father before he'd died. His total absorption in himself and meeting his own needs…and then the awful shock of seeing her with that man, the excoriating jealousy. Realising how much he'd lost sight of himself and who he was, who he had to be. Exactly what his father had warned him against.

Kaden strode over to the drinks cabinet, poured himself a measure of neat whisky and knocked it back. The burn made him reach for another one, as if that might douse the unquenchable desire, the tangled knot of feelings his wife so effortlessly evoked. He'd told himself that when he'd met her again in London he'd just wanted to bed her. And when she'd arrived to tell him about her pregnancy he'd thought only of the babies.

Now those assertions rang like the hollow untruths they were. Since he'd seen Julia again things had gone a lot deeper than he liked to admit.

The truth was, it was easier to avoid Julia and any chance of intimacy than face her and those grey eyes which made him feel as if he was coming apart at the seams every time he looked at her. Now more so than ever.

CHAPTER NINE

JULIA was trembling with nerves by the time they pulled up in Kaden's chauffeur-driven state car outside the hospital the following morning. She was dressed in a silvery grey long tunic, with matching pants underneath and a shawl to match. Her hair was tied back in a loose low bun, make-up and jewellery discreet. The tunic hid her pregnancy quite well—they'd agreed to wait another few days before making the announcement.

She took a deep shaky breath at the sight of the crowds amassed behind cordons, and then felt her hand being taken in a strong, warm grip. She almost closed her eyes for a second at the wave of longing that went through her. She turned to look at Kaden. His eyes were intent, compelling.

"I'll be right by your side. Just be yourself. They won't be able to help but respond to you."

"But I'm not a public person, Kaden… I've given speeches to rooms full of archaeologists, but never anything like this. They'll expect me to be something I'm not."

Something fierce crossed Kaden's face and he said, "They will accept you, Julia, because you're my wife and I've chosen you."

Julia felt sad, and pulled her hand away. She bit back the words trembling on her tongue. *You wouldn't have chosen me if you'd had a choice.*

Kaden's door was opened then, and with a last look he got out. The crowd went wild. He wore long cream robes and a traditional headdress. Julia's heart clenched amidst her trepidation. He reminded her so much in that moment of the young man she'd first met.

He was coming round the car. He'd instructed the driver to let him open her door. And then he was there, against the bright searing sun, holding out a hand. Julia took a deep breath and stepped out, clutching Kaden's hand. The roar of the crowd dipped ominously.

Security guards shadowed them as they walked towards the hospital. Julia tried to smile, but the crowd was blurring into a sea of faces that all looked suspiciously unfriendly. She was reminded of the aides who had surrounded Kaden after his father's death, when she hadn't been able to get close to him. She stumbled slightly and his arm came around her waist.

"OK?"

She looked up. "Yes, fine."

She drew on all her reserves as they got to the top of the steps and were greeted by officials from the hospital. They were exceedingly polite, but with a definite reserve. Kaden gave a short heartfelt speech about the new unit, which was specifically for heart disease, and then they turned towards the huge ribbon over the main doors.

Julia was handed a pair of scissors and cut it. Everyone clapped and cheered, but she couldn't help but notice the reticence of the crowd ever since she'd appeared at Kaden's side.

After being shown around inside by the doctors and officials they re-emerged, and Kaden led her towards the crowds. He said, "We'll do a short walkabout. It's expected."

Urged forward, Julia went towards a little girl, who pushed forward shyly to hold out some flowers. She bent down and took them, saying thank you in their native language. But Julia noticed the mother pull the child back, her lips pursed in disapproval, eyes dark and hard.

Another woman who held a baby visibly turned away, and adjusted a shawl over the baby's face so that Julia couldn't see it. As if to protect it from her gaze. Amongst her shock at the people's obvious rejection of her Julia felt a welling desire to have them look at her with open faces and smiles. She realised that she desperately wanted to be able to connect with them.

Kaden was taking her hand and pulling her back to the car. When they got in Julia was a little shell-shocked.

Kaden was grim as the car pulled away. "I'm sorry about that. They're wary after Amira and my stepmother...they'll come round."

"It's OK," Julia replied faintly, feeling more hurt than she'd thought possible. She'd not even known till then how important the Burquati people's opinion of her was. "I can understand that they wanted to see you with someone more suitable."

Kaden was silent beside her, and Julia didn't want to look at him and see disappointment in his second wife etched into his face.

When they got back to the palace Kaden stopped Julia and said, "I've got to go into the desert for a couple of days to meet with the newly elected Bedouin council."

Julia looked at him against the backdrop of the mag-

...icent central courtyard and felt a hollowness echoing through her. This was how it would be between them. Distance and polite civility.

She nodded. "Fine. I'll see you in a couple of days. I've got lessons to get on with in the meantime."

Julia turned away, and Kaden had an irrational urge to grab her back, throw her into the car and drive them far away. He wanted to be going into the desert with *her*, the way they'd used to. Sneaking off like fugitives, spending nights in a hastily erected tent under the stars. No thought in the world beyond exploring each other and sating mutual desire. And talking for hours.

An ache welled up inside him, and this time he couldn't ignore it. He had a sudden overwhelming need for those memories not to be tainted by what had happened twelve years before. For Julia to look at him the way she'd used to, with such open love and warmth. But the reality was clear. If Julia had ever had any feelings for him they were long gone. She was bound to him for ever, and she couldn't help but hate him for that. He'd seen the way that woman in the crowd had shielded her baby from Julia, as if she were some sort of witch. And Julia had just smiled.

With a jerky move, Kaden got back into the car which would take him to a helicopter to fly him into the desert. In that moment he'd never felt such bleakness surround him, and pain for subjecting Julia to the cold disapproval of his people when he knew just how deep her vulnerability went.

As Kaden flew over the desert a short time later the helicopter dipped abruptly for a moment in an air pocket. The pilot apologised and Kaden smiled tightly.

That physical sensation mirrored exactly how he fe emotionally, and it wasn't comfortable.

Julia spent the next two days working hard with her own secretary to encourage meetings with locals. She was determined to do what she could to bridge the gap, and wanted to avoid having any free time to brood about Kaden and the distance between them. She had to admit, though, that talking to him about her adoption had been cathartic. Thoughts of it and her birth mother no longer came with the heavy oppressive weight they'd used to.

To her delight she'd managed to set up a few coffee morning events at the palace, to meet with local women's groups and dicuss various issues. Julia had always had an interest in the more anthropological end of archaeology, so the prospect of meeting Burquati people and coming to learn their customs excited her.

She was in the middle of her first coffee morning when she saw Kaden again, and she nearly dropped her cup. He stood in the doorway, tall and gorgeous in long robes, jaw dark with stubble. He'd obviously just returned. She could swear her heart physically clenched as she saw him again.

All the women immediately bowed and went silent.

He inclined his head. "I'll leave you to it. I'm sure you're discussing far more important things than I will be at my cabinet meeting later."

He smiled, but to Julia it looked slightly strained. His eyes skated over her, giving her no more nor less attention than the other women. The awful yearning for him to acknowledge her with more than that inclusive glance nearly overwhelmed her, and she had to shove the hurt down deep.

He left, and after a moment of pregnant silence the women started chattering in a mixture of English and Burquati. Julia had been struggling to connect with the women, who'd seemed very suspicious, but suddenly they were all smiles and laughs.

Her secretary smiled at her sympathetically, misreading her anguish. "Don't worry. It'll just take some time."

Julia smiled wanly and went to join in again, feeling prickly because, if truth be told, she was jealous of these women. Kaden could come and charm them so effortlessly when he couldn't even be bothered to touch her any more!

Julia was lying in bed that night, unable to sleep. Kaden hadn't returned to their suite all evening, and she'd eaten dinner alone. She knew she couldn't continue like this, with Kaden holding her at arm's length and looking at her as if she might explode at any moment like a ticking bomb.

When she heard his familiar step she tensed. He came into the moonlit room, treading quietly.

Julia came up on one elbow and said huskily, "I'm awake."

He stopped, and all she could see in the gloom was his huge shape. Predictably, despite her tangled head and emotions, her body reacted to the sight of him. Softening, melting.

She sat up and pulled her knees towards her to try and hide her agitation. "Why didn't you come to dinner?"

Kaden started to disrobe. Julia could see gleaming flesh revealed bit by bit, and her belly clenched helplessly with desire.

His voice was cool. "I got held up with a phone call

to Sadiq, discussing the oil wells. They're expecting a baby too. Not long after us."

"Oh…" Julia didn't know what to say. Kaden seemed to be determined to avoid any further discussion.

He came to the bed and lifted back the covers, getting in and lying down. Tension vibrated between them like a tangible thing.

Julia turned to face him, feeling her hair slip over her shoulders. "Kaden…we need to talk. It's obvious that this isn't working out."

Kaden didn't like the flare of panic. He'd been reacting all day to the gut-wrenchingly urgent need he'd had to see Julia immediately on his return from the desert. And then, when he had seen her, the relief had sent him away again just as quickly, for fear she'd read something into his reaction that he didn't want her to see.

He felt as if he was clinging onto the last link that was rooting him in reality. That was rooting him in what he knew and had accepted for twelve long years. His distance from Julia for the past couple of days had restored some clarity, some perspective, and a sense that perhaps he wasn't going mad… Except earlier, and now, it was back with a vengeance. Any illusion of control gone.

His whole body was rigid against the effortless pull of Julia beside him. Her soft scent was like a siren's call to his blood. He turned his head and saw her outline: the slim shoulders, the curve of her breasts, the swell of her belly under the soft cotton of her vest. She wore vests and shorts to bed, attire he'd never seen another woman wear, and yet it inflamed him more than the slinkiest negligée he'd ever seen.

He turned away from temptation and forced out, "What isn't working out?"

His clear reluctance to talk made the tiny flame of hope Julia had harboured that they might discuss this fade away. She was overwhelmed for a moment by the sense of futility, and lay down too. She said in a small voice, "Nothing. It doesn't matter."

For a moment there was nothing but thick silence, and then, in a move so fast she gasped, Kaden was looming over her, eyes like black pools. "Tell me, Julia. What were you going to say?"

He was fierce, when only moments before his rigid control had been palpable. She smelt the slightest hint of whisky on his breath, and somehow suspecting that he was in some sort of turmoil too made her feel simultaneously tender and combative. And something in her exulted that he was finally reacting.

Before she could say anything, though, something in the atmosphere shifted and his fingers touched her throat. He said huskily, "You're wearing the necklace."

Julia froze all over, going clammy. Some of her things had arrived from London earlier and she'd found the necklace. She'd put it on, feeling some silly need to connect with something she'd always found comforting. She'd fully intended to take it off.

She immediately sought to protect herself from his scrutiny and drew back minutely. "It's OK. You don't have to get the wrong idea…"

His voice was a lot harsher than a moment ago. "What does it mean, Julia? Why have you kept it all this time?"

Julia knocked his hand away and scrambled inelegantly out of the bed, feeling far too vulnerable lying so close to a naked Kaden.

She lashed out in her own anger for exposing herself like this and in anger at Kaden for questioning her.

"I just saw it and put it on. It doesn't mean anything. It certainly doesn't mean that I don't know what this marriage is about. It's about the fact that I'm pregnant with your precious heirs—nothing more, nothing less."

Kaden uncoiled his big body from the bed and walked around to Julia. Acting on the irrational panic rising within her that she was about to come apart completely, Julia reached up and grabbed the necklace with her hand. She yanked at it, breaking the delicate chain instantly, and flung it aside onto the ground.

Inside she was weeping. Outwardly she hitched up her chin. "See? It means *nothing*."

Kaden looked at where she'd thrown the necklace and then back to her. The air crackled between them. In an abrupt move he pulled her into his body and said fiercely, "You don't have to resort to dramatics to make your point. I get the message. From now on there will be no doubt as to what this marriage is about."

Julia closed her eyes as Kaden's mouth fused to hers, his arms like a vice around her. Their bodies strained together. Tears burned the backs of her eyes, but she would not let Kaden see the helpless emotion. It was hot and overflowing, but as Kaden lowered her onto the bed and came down over her she shut her mind to all the mocking voices which told her that she was fooling no one but herself.

The following day Kaden was standing alone on an open terrace in the palace. He'd been having a meeting with an architect about the palace's preservation, but the architect had long gone. The city of Burquat was laid out before him. Cranes dotted the skyline—evidence of much necessary modernisation.

Kaden didn't see the view, though. His thoughts were inward. He smiled grimly to himself. He'd been right to fear touching Julia again. It was as if he'd known it would be the final catalyst in his coming undone. His own useless defence system had crashed and burned spectacularly last night, like a row of elaborate dominoes falling down with one small nudge.

Julia had only had to wear that necklace for him to see clearly for the first time in years.

His jaw tightened. Even then he hadn't been able to give in, still fighting right to the end… He'd had to make her say it, make her tell him how she really felt. As if he needed the concrete proof of her words and to feel the pain that came with them. Because he knew he deserved it. Perhaps that was what he'd been protecting himself against all along—the truth of *her* feelings. Not just his own.

He'd held something very precious a long time ago, and he'd broken it for ever. Kaden looked down and opened his fist to reveal the necklace, its chain in two pieces.

CHAPTER TEN

JULIA was in their private dining room, where Kaden had said he'd meet her for lunch. She was standing at the open French doors but seeing nothing of the glorious view. A couple of weeks had passed since that night. When Julia had woken the morning after she'd been alone. She'd immediately got up to look for the necklace but hadn't found it. Her sense of loss was profound, but she was too nervous to mention it to anyone or ask for help in searching for it. The last thing she wanted was for Kaden to know she was scrabbling around looking for it at any given opportunity.

She'd had to realise with a heavy heart that perhaps she needed to be rid of it because it symbolised something she'd never really had or would have—Kaden's love.

Kaden hadn't avoided her at night since then. They'd made love. And yet his touch was more…reticent. As if he was scared he'd hurt her. It seemed to compound the yawning chasm growing between them, so much worse than before.

How could they have gone three steps forward only to go about a hundred back?

"I'm sorry to have kept you waiting."

Julia whirled around to see Kaden in the doorway. Even though he'd left their bed only hours before, she blushed. She schooled her reaction and walked to the table. Just as she put out a hand to touch her chair she felt a kick in her womb, forcible enough to make her gasp and touch her bump, which was now big enough to be obvious to everyone.

Instantly Kaden was at her side, holding her arm. "What is it?"

As much in reaction to his touch as the kick, Julia said shakily, "I'm fine…it was just a kick—the first real kick I've felt."

Another one came then, and she couldn't stop a smile spreading across her face. Feeling the babies move was dissolving any inhibitions. She reached instinctively for Kaden's hand and brought it to her belly, pressing it down, praying that they would kick again. She looked at Kaden, and as always the ever-present awareness seemed to hum between them.

When the seconds stretched and there were no more kicks Julia flushed. She felt exposed. Kaden was too close, looking at her too assessingly. She pulled his hand away,

"They've stopped…"

Instantly the connection was broken, and Kaden stalked to the other side of the table and sat down. Staff appeared as if by magic and served them. Their conversation was stilted, centring around a charity fête that Julia was due to attend that afternoon.

When they'd finished eating Julia wiped her mouth, preparing to go.

Kaden said, "You don't have to go to the fête this afternoon if you don't want to. Unfortunately I can't get out of my meeting with the foreign minister. He's due to fly to the US tomorrow."

Julia smiled tightly. "It'll be fine. I need to get used to going to these things on my own sooner or later."

Kaden leaned forward and took her hand in his. Julia's eyes widened.

"I know this is hard for you, but already I can see a difference in people's attitudes. You're winning them round." He grimaced then. "I'm sorry that you have to go through this when you'd never have willingly signed up for this life."

Julia's face burned. Little did he know that she'd often dreamt of being by his side.

She took back her hand and pushed back her chair. "The car will be waiting."

Kaden watched her leave the room and cursed himself. He clenched his fist and just stopped himself from bringing it crashing down on the table. He kept thinking about the moment after their wedding, when he'd found her sobbing her heart out. Guilt burned in his gut, compounded now by the way he'd felt when he'd seen that beatific smile lighting up her face. He'd felt jealous that something else could make her happy. Jealous of his own babies!

The moment hadn't lasted long before she'd withdrawn again to that cool, polite distance which only dissolved when they were in bed.

He didn't need to be reminded that Julia hadn't smiled like that once since she'd met him again. As if he didn't know why. She was stuck in a marriage of convenience with a man who had brutally rejected her when she'd been at her most vulnerable just to protect his own cowardly heart. Julia was humbling him every day with her innate grace and stoic acceptance of a difficult situation. Of a life she didn't want.

Kaden knew that he had to be fully honest with her. She deserved to know everything. Later, he vowed. When she got home he would tell her. *Everything.* And whatever her reaction was…he would have to deal with it.

Two hours later Kaden was sitting at his desk listening to his minister for foreign affairs talk, but not taking anything in. He was wondering where Julia was now. Had she reached the fête? Was she feeling awkward? Was she smiling in that slightly fixed way which signified she was shy or uncomfortable? His gut clenched at the thought of anyone being rude or unfriendly to her.

Only last week he'd watched her host another of her coffee mornings, this time outside in the palace grounds. He'd been inordinately proud of the way she'd listened to people, really devoting her time to them. A million miles away from his ex-wife and stepmother who had both been brought up specially schooled to be in this world.

"Sire?"

They'd announced the news of Julia's pregnancy a few days ago, now that she was showing more obviously, and he was hoping it would have an effect on people's interaction with her. Surely the prospect of—?

"Sire!"

"Hmm?" Kaden looked at his minister, a little dazed for a moment, and then saw that his secretary was also in the room. He frowned. He hadn't even noticed her come in. "Yes, Sara?"

He only noticed then that she was deathly pale and

trembling. The hair went up on the back of his neck for no reason.

"Sire, I'm sorry to disturb you, but I've just heard—there's been a terrible multi-vehicle accident on the main freeway to Kazat, where the fête is. We've been trying to call your wife and the driver, but there's no response from them or the bodyguards. We don't have news yet as the emergency services haven't reached them."

Kaden heard her words and tried to react, to move. But it was as if his limbs were instantly weighted down with wet cement. He couldn't get up. He could feel his blood draining south and put his hands on his desk to hold on to something.

His secretary started crying and the foreign minister stood up. "Sire, I'll get your car immediately."

Kaden stood up then, even though he couldn't feel his own legs, and said with an icy calm which belied the roaring in his brain, "Not the car. Too slow. Get the helicopter ready and make sure there's a doctor and a paramedic on board. *Now*."

What felt like aeons later, but what was in fact only thirty minutes, Kaden's helicopter pilot was setting down in a clearing beside the freeway. All Kaden could see was a tangled mass of vehicles, a school bus on its side, with steam billowing out of its engine, and lines of cars blocking the freeway.

The flashing lights of the first emergency vehicles were evident, and there were people blackened from smoke and fire rushing everywhere. And amongst all that twisted metal and heat was Julia. Kaden's mind shut down and he went into autopilot. He simply could not contemplate anything beyond the next few seconds.

The blast of heat nearly pushed him backwards

when he got out of the chopper, but Kaden ignored it and waded straight into the carnage. He shouted at the young, scared-looking doctor with him, "Stay beside me!"

All around them people were wandering around looking dazed, with blood running down their faces, holding hands and arms. But to Kaden's initial and fleeting relief there seemed no serious-looking injuries. He focused on the school bus on its side, and as he went towards it, acting on instinct, he finally saw the Royal car. It was skewed at an angle near the bus, ploughed into the steel girder which ran down the middle of the highway, and near it, on its roof, was the security Jeep.

Kaden's heart stopped. He ran towards the car, and when he got there, his lungs burning, ducked his head into the back seat. It was empty. He felt sick when he saw the trail of blood that led out of the car.

He stood up. *"Julia!"*

Nothing. Panic at full throttle now, he went towards the other side of the school bus and stopped dead in his tracks, a mixture of overwhelming relief and incoherent rage making him dizzy. Julia was handing a small child to her driver, who was in turn handing it to someone else. Adults who looked like teachers were standing in groups with other children, crying. Julia's kaftan was ripped and bloody.

He went towards her and she saw him. "Oh, Kaden—thank God! Please…you have to help us. There are still some children trapped inside, and the engine is leaking petrol."

She looked half crazed, which he could see was due to shock and adrenalin, and in the periphery of his vision he could see people standing with phones, taking videos and photos. Very deliberately he put his hands on Julia's arms and bodily moved her out of harm's way. He looked at the doctor and said, "She's over five months pregnant. If anything happens to her you'll be held personally responsible."

Julia protested. "But, Kaden, there are still children—"

He cut her off. "*You* stay here. *I* will go and get the children. If you move one inch, Julia, so help me God I will lock you in the palace for the rest of your life."

Through a haze of shock and panic Julia could only feel limp with relief as she watched Kaden stride back to the bus, climb up, and reach in to help pull the children out. Within minutes they were all accounted for, and Julia had already instructed the now terrified-looking doctor to go and help the injured children instead of babysitting her. She was helping too, ripping material off her dress to tie around bleeding arms and legs.

She felt herself being lifted upwards and was turned into Kaden's chest. His eyes burned down into hers. "Are you OK? Are you in pain anywhere?"

Julia shook her head. Some of the shock was starting to wear off, so she was aware of how deranged Kaden looked. She put it down to the accident. "I'm fine. We need to help these people…"

But her words were muffled against Kaden's chest as he pulled her into him and hugged her so tightly that she couldn't breathe. Eventually he pulled back. "We're getting out of here right now. I need to get you to the hospital."

Julia protested. "I'm fine—what about all these people? The children? They need help more than me!"

But Kaden wasn't listening. She could see an emergency medical plane circling overhead, and more choppers landing. The scene was swarming with emergency staff now, and the young doctor was busy.

When she still resisted, Kaden uttered an oath and turned and picked her up into his arms. Julia opened her mouth, but closed it again at the stern set of his features. He looked as if he was going to murder someone, and she felt a pang when she recalled what he'd said to the doctor. *"She's over five months pregnant..."* He must be livid with her for putting their babies at risk.

She was in the chopper and secured within minutes, and then they were lifting up and away from the mayhem. Julia was comforted to see that the emergency vehicles were already speeding back towards the city, and other choppers were loading up with patients.

Kaden couldn't speak because of the noise but Julia was glad. She wasn't looking forward to what he had to say.

"Kaden, why don't you just spit it out? You're giving me a headache, pacing around like a bear with a sore head."

He stopped and glared at her, his jeans and shirt ripped and dusty. "You're a national hero. Do you know that? With one fell swoop the entire nation is in love with you."

"What do you mean?" Julia was confused.

Kaden picked up the remote and turned on the TV. A rolling news channel was showing images of the crash, and then it zoomed in on Julia, where she was handing a small child to someone.

She glanced at Kaden. He'd gone grey.

He switched the TV off and muttered thickly, "I can't even watch that."

Tears stung Julia's eyes. "I'm sorry, but I couldn't just ignore what was happening. I know these babies are important to you, but surely your own people are important too?"

He just looked at her. "What are you talking about?"

Julia put her hand on her bump. She'd just had a scan with Dr Assan and been reassured that all was fine. "The babies. I presume that's why you're so angry with me… for putting them in danger?"

Kaden raked a hand through his hair and ground out, "I'm not angry with you for putting the babies in danger. I'm *livid* with you for putting *yourself* in such danger."

He came close before Julia could fully take in his words and sat down, pulling a chair close to the bed and taking her hands in his with a tight grip. "Do you have any idea what I went through before I got to you?"

Julia shook her head slowly. An ominous fluttering feeling was starting up in her chest.

"I think I aged about fifty years, and made blood promises to several gods. So if some strange-looking person turns up and demands our firstborn baby don't be surprised."

"Kaden…" Julia was feeling more shaky now than when she'd been at the crash. "What are you talking about? You're not making sense." And yet at the same time he was making a kind of sense she didn't want to think about.

"What I'm talking about, *habiba*, is the fact that for the longest thirty minutes of my life I didn't want to go on living if anything had happened to you."

Feeling suspiciously emotional, and very vulnerable, Julia couldn't take her eyes off Kaden.

He continued. “I was going to talk to you this evening when you got back…I don’t want to tire you now…”

Concern was etched onto his face, and Julia said fiercely, “I’m fine. Talk.”

Kaden looked down, and then back up at Julia. “I’m not sure where to start… There’s so much I have to say… But I think first I need to tell you the one truth that is more important than anything.”

Julia held her breath as Kaden gripped her hand tighter.

“I want you to know that I’m not saying this now because of the crash, or because of the after effects of adrenalin and shock. I had arranged for us to go to the summer palace this evening, for a belated honeymoon. You can ask Sara. She was organising it.”

“Kaden…” Julia said weakly. She couldn’t look away from the dark intensity of his eyes.

He took a deep, audibly shaky breath. “I love you, Julia. Mind, body, heart and soul. And I always have. From the moment we met in the middle of that dig. I did a wonderful job of convincing myself twelve years ago that I hadn’t ever loved you, but as soon as I saw you again the game was up…and eventually I had to stop lying to myself.”

Julia looked at Kaden in shock. She could hear her heart thumping. Her mouth opened.

Kaden shook his head and said, “Don’t say anything—not yet. Let me finish.”

Julia couldn’t have spoken, even if she’d wanted to. Her mouth closed. She could feel the babies moving in her belly, but that was secondary to what was happening right now.

“The day you left twelve years ago was possibly the

worst day of my life." He winced. "Barring today's events. I felt as if I was being torn in two—like Jekyll and Hyde. For a long time I blamed the grief I felt on my father's death—and that was there, yes. But a larger part of my grief was for you. There's something I have to explain. When we returned from that last trip to the desert I went to my father. I told him that I was going to ask you to marry me. All I could think about was you—you filled up my heart and soul like nothing I'd ever imagined, and I couldn't imagine not being with you for ever."

Julia could feel herself go pale as she remembered that heady time. And then her confusion when Kaden had abandoned her. She shook her head. "But why did you not come to see me? Tell me this…?"

Kaden's jaw clenched. "Because that night my father had his first heart attack. Only those closest to him knew how serious it was. We sent out the news that he wasn't well, but we hid the gravity of the situation for fear of panicking the people. I became acting ruler overnight. I was constantly surrounded by aides. I couldn't move two steps without being questioned or followed. And I suspect that after what I'd told my father he instructed his aides to keep an eye on me and not let me near you.

"I think he saw history repeating itself. His second wife had been a bad choice, unpopular with the people. He knew how important it would be for me to marry well and create a stable base, and here I was declaring my intention to ask *you* to marry me and to hell with the consequences."

Kaden sighed. "I stuck to my guns. I was still determined to ask you to marry me. I decided that while you were finishing your studies I'd give you the time to think about whether or not you really wanted this life..."

Julia felt tears prickle at the back of her eyes. She knew how she would have answered that.

Kaden's voice was gruff. "The first chance I had I got away on my own and went to find you. One of your tutors told me you were all out that night in a bar..."

Julia squeezed Kaden's hand, willing him to believe her. "You have to know what you saw meant nothing...it was just a stupid kiss. It was over the moment it started. I was feeling insecure because I hadn't heard from you, and I think I wanted to assure myself that you couldn't be the only man who could make me feel. I was afraid we were over and I'd never see you again."

To Julia's intense relief Kaden picked up her hand and kissed her palm. "I know that now...and I can see how vulnerable you must have felt—especially so soon after that blow from your birth mother..." He grimaced. "I, however, was blindingly jealous and hot-headed. It felt like the ultimate betrayal. Especially when I'd been pining for you for what felt like endless nights, dreaming of proposing to you even if it meant going against my father's wishes. And then to see you in another man's arms...it was too much. The jealousy was overwhelming. I'd been brought up to view romantic love suspiciously. My father became a shadow of himself after my mother died, and he never stopped telling me that my duty was first and foremost to my country. He was most likely trying to protect me...but when I felt so betrayed by you it only seemed to confirm his words. I convinced myself that it wasn't love I felt. It was lust. Because then it wouldn't hurt so much."

Kaden shook his head. "I returned to the palace and

that night my father had his final heart attack. I got to him just before he slipped away, and his last words to me were pleas to remember that I was responsible for a country now, and had to look beyond my own personal fulfilment. By then I was more than ready to listen to him."

"Oh, Kaden…I had no idea." Pain cut through Julia as she saw how the sequence of events had played out with a kind of sickening synchronicity.

Kaden let her hands go and stood up, pacing away from Julia, self-disgust evident in every jerky movement. He turned round and looked haunted. "When you came to me before you left and tried to explain you got the full lash of my guilt and jealousy. I couldn't be rational. All I could see was you and that man. It haunted me even when we met again. The depth of the feelings I had for you always scared me a little, and I never resolved them years ago. I buried them, and that's why it took me so long to come to my senses…"

Julia felt incredibly sad. "We were so young, Kaden. Maybe we were just too young to cope with those feelings."

Kaden raked a hand through his hair. "That's why Samia looked at you with such hostility at her wedding. She was protecting me because she was the only one who saw the dark place I went to after you left. I never explained anything to her, so she assumed you'd broken my heart. When in fact I did a pretty good job of breaking yours."

"And your own…" Julia bit her lip to try and keep a lid on the overwhelming feelings within her. Tears blurred her vision, and despite her best efforts a sob broke free.

Kaden was standing apart, hands clenched at his sides, looking tortured.

She shook her head. "I just…I can't believe you're saying all this…" Another sob came out and she put a hand to her mouth. Tears were flowing freely down her face now.

Kaden clearly wanted to comfort her, but was holding back because he didn't know if she wanted him. "God, Julia…I'm so sorry. What I've done is—"

"Kaden, don't say anything else. Just hold me, please."

Julia wasn't even sure if her words had been entirely coherent, but Kaden moved forward jerkily, and after a moment he was sitting on the bed and enveloping her in his strong embrace.

Julia's hands were clenched against his chest. She couldn't stop crying, and kept thinking of all those wasted years and pain. Ineffectually she hit at his chest, and he tensed and pulled her even closer, as if to absorb her turmoil. Eventually he drew back and looked down, his face in agony. Seeing that made something dissolve inside Julia.

"Don't let me go, Kaden…"

He shook his head and said fiercely, "Never. I'll never let you go ever again."

When the paroxysm of emotion had abated Julia pulled back in the circle of his arms and said shakily, "I've always loved you. I never stopped. You and no one else. From the moment I saw you again in London all the feelings rushed back as if we'd never even been separated."

Kaden shook his head, clearly incredulous. "How can you? After everything… You don't have to say this…

You don't want to be here. You've been forced into this life."

Julia touched his face and smiled tremulously. "I wouldn't want to be anywhere else in the world. I was resigned to my fate, loving you while knowing you'd never love me back."

Kaden's eyes shone suspiciously. "Oh, my love…that's what *I* expected. I love you so much that if anything had happened to you today…"

He went pale again, and the full enormity of what Kaden had gone through hit Julia when she thought of how *she* would have felt if their places had been switched.

Fervently she said, "Let's go home, Kaden. I want to go home with you and start living the rest of our lives together. I don't want to waste another moment."

EPILOGUE

Seven months later

JULIA and Kaden were hosting a christening for their twins and for Samia and Sadiq's baby son, who was just a few weeks younger than the twins. The ceremony had finished in the ancient chapel in the grounds of the archaeological dig site. Julia was standing with Samia now, and they were watching Kaden cradle his dark-haired baby daughter Rihana with all the dexterity of a natural. His brother-in-law Sadiq was holding his son Zaki with similar proficiency.

Samia and Julia's first proper meeting had been awkward, but as soon as Kaden had set Samia straight she'd rounded on him and castigated him for letting her think the worst of Julia for years. Now they were fast becoming good friends.

"No doubt they're discussing the merits of eco-friendly nappies," Samia said dryly.

Julia snorted. "Kaden nearly fainted earlier when he smelt Tariq's morning deposit."

Samia giggled and linked arms with Julia. They'd just been made godmothers to each other's babies. "Come on—let me introduce you properly to Iseult and

Jamilah. You'll love them. Jamilah, the dark-haired one, is Salman's wife. She's got an inner beauty to match her outer beauty, which makes it annoyingly hard to hate her."

Julia chuckled. She'd only been briefly introduced to Sheikh Nadim of Merkazad and his stunningly pretty red-haired wife, and his brother Salman and *his* wife Jamilah. Both couples also had babies, who were crawling or toddling around, being chased by one or other of their parents.

Just as they approached the other women, though, Kaden cut in and handed Rihana to Samia. "Here you go, Auntie. I'm stealing my wife for a minute."

Samia took her baby niece eagerly. "Be careful—you might not get her back. And I think Tariq has already been stolen by Dr Assan."

They'd made Dr Assan their son's godfather, and he was showing him off like a proud grandfather.

Kaden took Julia's hand and led her out through a side door. He was dressed in gold and cream ceremonial robes, and Julia wore a cream silk dress. She let herself be led by Kaden through the shade of the old trees to the other side of the dig, feeling absurdly happy and content.

Kaden glanced back and smiled. "What are you looking so smug about?"

Julia smiled mysteriously, her heart full. "Oh, nothing much."

Kaden growled. "I'll make you tell me later, but first…"

They'd reached the corner, and Julia recognised the spot where they'd first met. Kaden brought her over to the ancient wall, and it took a moment before she could see what he was directing her attention to. A new stone had been placed amongst the older ones, and it held within it a fossil and an inscription.

She gasped and looked at him. "That's not the same fossil—?"

He smiled. "Read the writing."

She did. The inscription simply read: *For my wife and only love, Julia. You hold my heart and soul, as I will hold yours, for ever. Kaden*

It also had the date of the day they'd met. She looked at Kaden, feeling suspiciously teary, and saw that he was holding out his palm. She looked down and saw a familiar chain of gold. Her necklace. She picked it up reverently.

He sounded gruff. "I got it mended after that night."

Julia's eyes had filled with proper tears now, and Kaden said mock sternly, with his hands cupping her face and jaw, "I won't have tears marking this spot."

Julia smiled through the tears. "Kiss me, then, and make me happy."

"That," Kaden said, with love in his eyes and on his face, "I can most definitely do."

And so they kissed, for a long time, on the exact spot where they'd first met almost thirteen years before.

* * * * *

A sneaky peek at next month...

MODERN™

INTERNATIONAL AFFAIRS, SEDUCTION & PASSION GUARANTEED

My wish list for next month's titles...

In stores from 16th December 2011:

- ❑ The Man Who Risked It All – Michelle Reid
- ❑ The End of her Innocence – Sara Craven
- ❑ Secrets of Castillo del Arco – Trish Morey
- ❑ Untouched by His Diamonds – Lucy Ellis

In stores from 6th January 2012:

- ❑ The Sheikh's Undoing – Sharon Kendrick
- ❑ The Talk of Hollywood – Carole Mortimer
- ❑ Hajar's Hidden Legacy – Maisey Yates
- ❑ The Secret Sinclair – Cathy Williams
- ❑ Say It with Diamonds – Lucy King

Available at WHSmith, Tesco, Asda, Eason, Amazon and Apple

Visit us Online

You can buy our books online a month before they hit the shops! **www.millsandboon.co.uk**